Ten Weeks into COVID-19

Psyche, Money and Narratives
An interpretation of the crisis

By the same Author
published by Economica

Carnets monétaires, 2008.

Généalogie de l'économique, 2008.

Tractatus economico-philosophicus, 2008.

Valeur et temps – Essais économiques, 2008.

Théorie globale de l'intérêt, du cycle et de la mémoire, 2009.

La dynamique boursière – Les fondements, 2009.

Histoire du musicien à l'âge moderne – Musique, cité et politique, 2009.

Théorie du Sujet économique, 2010.

Money, Memory and Asset Prices, 2010.

L'économie sociale de la liberté, 2011.

The Social Economy of Freedom, 2011.

Grammatica Economica – Lecture de Keynes, Friedman et Hayek, 2012.

La Valeur – Substance, échange et prix, 2012.

Philosophy in Economics, 2nd edition, 2015 (first published in 2012).

The Economic and Financial Order, 2018.

Essays in Positive Investment Management, 3rd edition, 2019 (first published in 2014).

Valeur, Temps et Capital – Une théorie de l'économie évolutive, 2019.

Value, Time and Capital – A Theory of Progressive Economy, 2019.

Théorie pure du temps économique – Méditations rovelli-simoniennes, 2020.

Pure Theory of Economic Time – Rovelli-Simonian meditations, 2020.

Pascal Blanqué

Ten Weeks into COVID-19

Psyche, Money and Narratives
An interpretation of the crisis

ECONOMICA
49, rue Héricart, 75015 Paris

Printed in France
Ten Weeks into Covid-19
Psyche, Money and Narratives. An interpretation of the crisis
ISBN 978-2-7178-7218-7

We are grateful to Mrs Melanie Lanoë for the translation.

Foreword

This publication is first and foremost an observation, conducted during ten weeks of lockdown in France, which started on 13 March 2020. As such, it is a logbook, completed as the days and weeks passed.

It is also a theoretical endeavour to interpret, explain or recount the eruption of the crisis – it is these very first weeks which are of interest, as they contain the maximum intensity of the real, financial and psychological shock, in the form of a DNA for what follows.

This theoretical endeavour makes it possible to test, against the reality of the crisis, a certain number of hypotheses made in earlier works and to consolidate and refine our tool box.

The Covid-19 crisis offers a unique case-study for a theory which is concerned with the analogy between the circulation of viruses and that of money, images and narratives.

This period also reveals a notable gap, which is rapidly described as irrational, between the traditional, accepted view of fundamentals and the prices observed on the financial markets.

The term "irrational" is used to denote a difficulty or failure to understand a certain idea of posited rationality, especially when defined ex ante*. This may be due to an imperfect or incorrect interpretation of a relevant subject. Or, on the contrary, it may indicate that the matter under consideration is not relevant. It is, therefore, necessary to reformulate the fundamentals, as a function of subjective value and narration.*

PART I

Case study

INTRODUCTION – THE PROJECT

The Covid-19 crisis on the financial markets allows us to observe, in real-time or *in situ*, certain mechanisms for the formation of anticipations which we described notably in *Money, Memory and Asset Prices.*

The variation in prices can be explained by the memory of war sequences (the vocabulary used in the crisis often refers to a state of war; such as, in March, at the time of the announcement of the lockdown, the reference to June 1940 and the exodus, when over one million people left the *Ile de France* region in a period of just two weeks) and of former pandemics (the Spanish flu in 1921).

Connected to these sequences is a return of emotions and an objectivation of the benchmark situations (number of deaths, duration of the epidemic...) which are used for comparison or reference purposes.

One cannot help but be struck by what is, literally, an irruption of, or a return to, lexical registers (war, historical pandemics) which structure the language and the description or analysis of what is real.

The psychological time referential is distorted. One moves more or less quickly, the more or less one remembers (or forgets). There is an acceleration of psychological time.

(Maximum) forgetfulness, which was a feature of the top of the cycle, in particular the peak in financial asset prices, is replaced by a sudden memory recall of such “patterns” (structures, sequences) (the strict counterpart of which is the act of forgetting the very top of the cycle itself and its structure).

By way of method, observation of the evolution of the Covid crisis makes it possible to identify (i) a few pointers for the estimation of certain important variables in our description, such as Mr (the rate of memory recall) and Fr (the rate of forgetting) and (ii) recurrences and frequencies of patterns, images and lexical forms within all the narratives (of images and discourses); once an image-object (io) is identified, the rate of its presence and persistence can be estimated.

Moreover, the crisis offers an opportunity to observe a real and very significant case of monetary action (including considerable quantitative easings or QE) and the greater or lesser impact of its trajectory.

We refer here to our work (*Essays in Positive Investment Management*; *Théorie globale de l’intérêt, du cycle et de la mémoire*), in which we posited the principal hypothesis that an increase in money supply (in order to stylise the whole of the monetary actions) will only have an impact on activity and prices, if there is a distortion of the psychological referential (the psychological velocity of money, which is literally imprinted by memory, forgetting and duration). A fall in asset prices can initially be seen, which continues whilst the money supply increases (the referential is still dominated by the sequences and structures which were unexpectedly recalled) (see above).

We posited that QE would literally make it possible to “buy time”, since it would allow for (?) or be accompanied by (?) a modification in the psychological referential with an elongation of psychological time. The expansion (or contraction) of the money supply is consistent with various states of psychological time. We can use this to infer the sorts of indifference or efficiency curves. This work is outlined in *Essays in Positive Investment Management*.

CHAPTER 1

Weeks 1 & 2
The various states of the psychological time referential

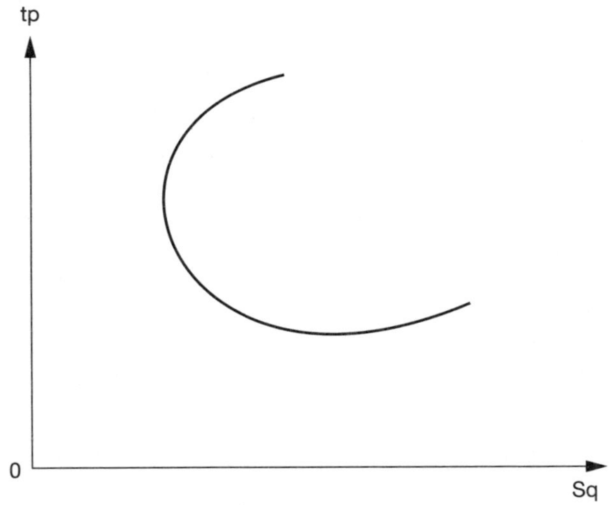

FIGURE 1. *Psychological time and stock of money*

We are, therefore, trying to see, within the crisis, whether there are observable indications of a distortion of the referential and, consequently, of psychological time.

SEQUENCES AND DEFINITIONS

There is indeed a change in Sq, which moves from Sq_0 to Sq_1 with the numerous monetary initiatives of the central banks (lower rates, balance sheet expansions, various quantitative easings...).

We have tp_0 which characterises the psychological referential at the top of the cycle. The sequence is as follows:

t_{phy}	t_{phy}	Asset prices	M/F	t_{psy}	(m)	Cycle Fi	$(Vm)_{psy} = (Vm)_R$	$(Vm)_{Fi}$	$(Vm)_{Re}$	Cycle Re	(N_{Fi}, N_{Re})
t_0	01-20	↗↔	Fmax	(↘ min max)	↗	Top of cycle	↘ min	↗	↗	Middle of cycle ↗	(++, ++)
t_1	03-20	↓	M↗	↗↗	↗↗	↓	↗↗	↘↘	↘	↓	(−−, −−)
t_2	03-20	↓	M↗	↗↗	↗↗	↓	↗↗	↘↘	↘	↓	(+, −+)
t_3	04-20	↘	M↗	↗↗	↗↗	↓	↗↗	↘↘	↘	↓	(+, −+)
t_4	04-20	↗	M ↗↘	↗↗	↗↗	→↗	↗	↘	↘↘	↓↓	(++, −)
t_5	04-20	↗	M↓ ↗↘	→	↗↗	→↗	→↘	→	↘↘	↓↓	(++, −)
t_6	04-20	↗	M↓ ↗↘	→	↗↗	→↗	↗	↗	↘↘	↓↓	(++, +)
t_7	05-20	↗↔	M↓	↘	↗↗	↗	↘	↗	↘	↓↓	(+, −+)
t_8	05-20	↗↔	M↓	↘	↗↗	↗	↘	↗	↘	↓↓	(+, −+)
t_9	05-20	↗↔	M↓	↘	↗↗	↗	↘	↗	↘	↓↓	(+, −)
t_{10}	05-20	↗↔	M↓	↘	↗↗	↗	↘	↗	↘	↓↓	(+, −)

FIGURE 2. *General overview of the 10-week period*

Psychological time and psychological velocity of money

We define (i) a psychological time, noted as t_{psy} and (ii) a psychological velocity of money, noted as Vm_{psy}.

(i) t_{psy} is defined within the psychological referential structured by memory, forgetting and duration (M/F, D). We have posited (see *Money, Memory and Asset Prices*; *Essays in Positive Investment Management; Value, Time and Capital*; *Pure Theory of Economic Time*) that one moved more quickly (slowly) within the referential the more (or less) intensely one remembered or forgot, by freeing oneself from the chronologies of clock-time. For example, the abrupt and rapid return (in the sense of physical time) of distant memory structures (patterns) during the Covid crisis (the 1939-45 war; the 1921 Spanish flu; but also of more distant patterns, such as the mediaeval Black Death) represents an acceleration of psychological time (a contraction of the psychological time referential) based on a situation with a very high level of forgetfulness. This phenomenon is noted $t_{psy}\uparrow_C$ (as compared to a deceleration movement with a dilation of psychological time within the referential, *i.e.* $t_{psy}\downarrow_D$.)

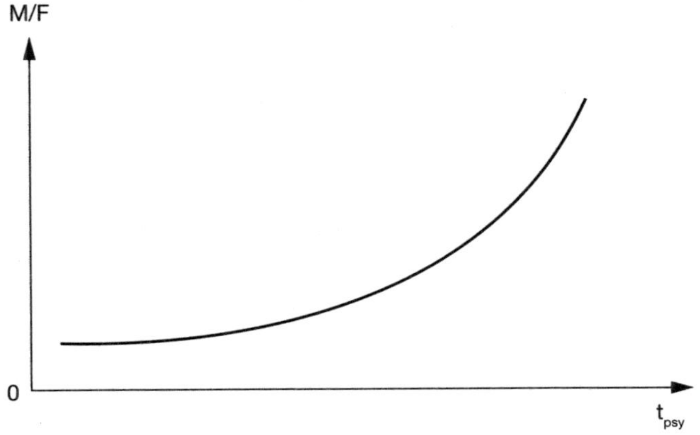

FIGURE 3. *Psychological time, memory and forgetfulness*

Psychological time is at its maximum, as it were, when M or F are themselves at their maximum.

We have here a standard situation, where there is a sudden memory recall starting from a very high rate of forgetting.

The rate of memory recall is higher, if the rate of forgetting was higher, *i.e.* the elongation of psychological time was more substantial.

We can thus advance that:

- the rate of memory recall Mr rises with a contraction of the temporal, psychological referential R;
- the rate of forgetting Fr rises with a dilation of the temporal, psychological referential R;
- Mr is at its maximum when close to the maximum of Fr and vice versa.

(ii) The psychological velocity of money (Vm_{psy}) is based on the hypothesis made in the reference works cited above, *i.e.* that a change in the money supply can only have an effect on activity or prices, if certain configurations of the psychological referential R are put in place, *i.e.* (M/F, D) (see *Théorie globale de l'intérêt, du cycle et de la mémoire*; *Money, Memory and Asset Prices*). Money is, as it were, imprinted by R and M/F. We are therefore seeking, within the context of the Covid crisis, to observe, within (physical) time, the links between money supply (as a proxy for monetary easing) and the parameters of the referential.

Money may circulate within the real sphere or within the financial sphere, and this circulation may thus represent the intensity of real or financial transactions per monetary unit. These observable variables are accompanied by a non-observable variable, Vm_{psy}.

The acceleration of psychological time t_{psy} has been defined above as a contraction of the psychological referential R (the example we gave is a sudden and intense memory recall after an intensity of forgetting which is also strong). The psychological velocity of money increases with the acceleration of psychological time – psychological time contracts, in fact reflects a contraction of the psychological referential. A greater, temporal, psychological intensity enters per monetary unit, which means here more memory returning in an abrupt and intense manner. The intensity of memory recall in the example observed in the Covid crisis coincides with an increase in Vm_{psy}.

The intensity of memory or forgetting per monetary unit

The intensity of memory or forgetting per monetary unit (for each transaction) constitutes one way of approaching Vm_{psy}. This is how one defines configurations of an increase or decrease in Vm_{psy} which are not necessarily consistent with comparable configurations of an increase or decrease in the velocity of m within the real and financial spheres.

In fact, when the rate of forgetting is at its maximum, the psychological rate decelerates, there is a dilation of the psychological referential and the psychological velocity of money itself slows down, *i.e.* the contents of memory per monetary unit for a transaction decrease until they ultimately disappear. At that moment, the velocity of money within the financial sphere accelerates up to a maximum point at the top of the cycle, whether or not accompanied (since the two velocities may be disconnected) by an increase in the velocity of m within the real sphere.

At the top of the market cycle (January 2020) (which does not then correspond to the top of the real cycle – there is then a form of acceleration of the real economy within a configuration of the end or prolonged middle of the cycle), there is a rise in velocity and a high level of velocity of m within the financial sphere (m is high and rising; the rate of forgetting is high and increasing; Vm_{psy} is low, since the rate of forgetting is at its maximum: there is almost no more circulation within the psychological referential R and its imaginary world).

In the phase which immediately follows, the fall of the markets goes hand in hand with a fall in the velocity of m within the financial sphere, which corresponds to an increase of Vm_{psy} through the memory recall of referential structures within the economy and the markets. m is high and increasing but there is a deflationary shock, *i.e.* a decline in the velocities of m within the real and financial spheres, against the background of a rise in the psychological velocity of m through an abrupt memory recall, *i.e.* an acceleration of the movement within R as compared to a tranquil situation of lethargy, as it were, imposed by the act of forgetting (deceleration of psychological time, dilation of R).

The additional increase in m, which then occurs as a result of the monetary actions by the central banks, does not prevent the velocities of m within the real and financial spheres from continuing to fall. This is consistent with a continuous acceleration of Vm_{psy}, *i.e.* whilst R is driven by an intensity of memory movements.

PSYCHOLOGICAL TIME AND THE POSITIVE OR NEGATIVE STRUCTURES OF MEMORY

We may wonder which is the *more* important as between:

(i) the movement (t_{psy}) within the referential R which, in our description, is caused by M, as opposed to forgetting which elongates t_{psy}; and

(ii) the positive or negative, as it were, nature of the structure which constitutes memory recall. In this instance, they are negative structures (war, Spanish flu, plague), in the sense that they steer the markets and the economy downwards.

Consequently, an upward trend in Vm_{psy} with positive structures may be linked to an increase in the velocities of m within the real and financial spheres.

A decrease in the velocities of m within the real and financial spheres at the start of the crisis corresponds, in our hypothesis, to an increase in Vm_{psy}, with a return of a dominant, negative memory pattern (the Spanish flu pandemic, war). To be precise: what is essential and of overriding importance, is the very fact that there is a memory recall, based on a high rate of forgetting, which in our hypothesis corresponds to a form of lethargic, level surface. It is the setting (back) into motion which makes the difference.

Moreover, there is the issue of the patterns of M, the structures and image-objects which make up the substance and form of this projection of consciousness represented by memory recall. Although, as the crisis erupts, the image-objects, which literally come to mind, have something to do with past wars or pandemics, they are not the only ones, since numerous other image-objects inhabit the structure or are called upon within the new sequence.

We therefore formulate a hypothesis that the psychological velocity of money is at its minimum (collapses) at the extreme points of forgetting, *i.e.* when the speed of movement (in short, the movement itself) is at its minimum within the psychological referential.

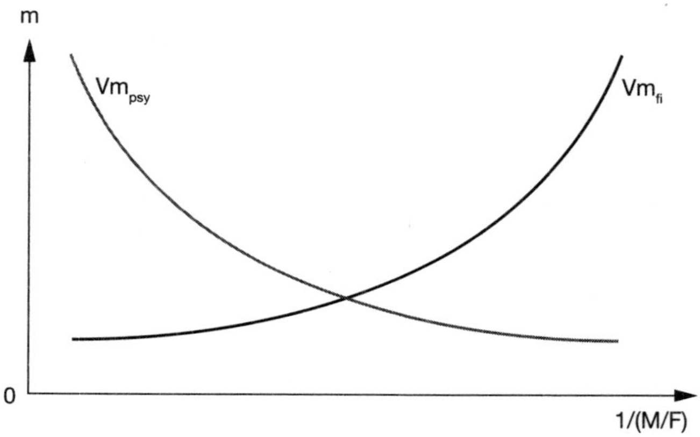

FIGURE 4. *Psychological and financial velocities of money*

These extreme sequences of forgetting correspond to sequences of a rise or acceleration in the velocities of money within the financial sphere (bubble) and real sphere (inflation in the traditional sense of the price of goods and services) (note that these two forms of velocity are not necessarily correlated, even if, in certain conditions, one may be accompanied by the other or may lead to the other).

Accordingly, in order that an increase in money supply might be accompanied by an ultimate impact on activity and on (real and financial) prices – which involves an increase in the velocities of m within the financial and real spheres – the psychological velocity of money has to be low (Vm_{psy}), *i.e.* the level of activity within the psychological referential must itself be low.

The increase in activity in R, which represents a rise in movements within the psychological space-time, coincides with the phenomena of memory recalls and, therefore, an increase in the psychological velocity of money (Vm_{psy}). The increase in (Vm_{psy}), even though the supply of money remains high or is increased, is accompanied by a decrease in the velocities of real and financial m. This is what is suggested by an observation of the crisis.

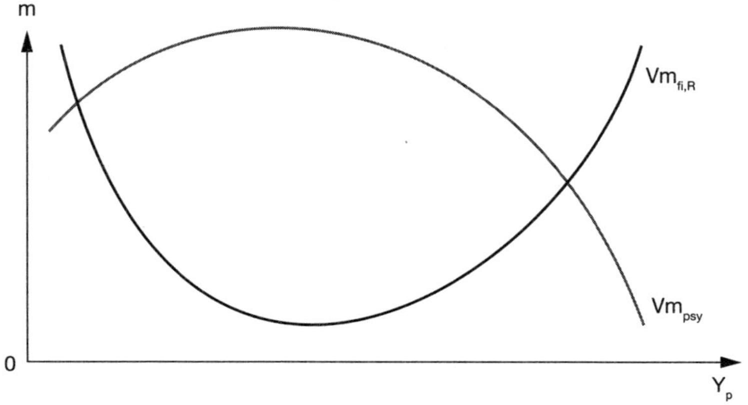

FIGURE 5. *Velocities of money, activity and price*

where Y = activity
p = price

It can be seen that a high level of money supply is not enough to ensure an increase in activity (Y) and in prices in the broad sense (p). The region where m is high but where Vm_{psy} is also high does not make it possible to attain levels of Y and p which are themselves high, even if the real and financial velocities of money are high.

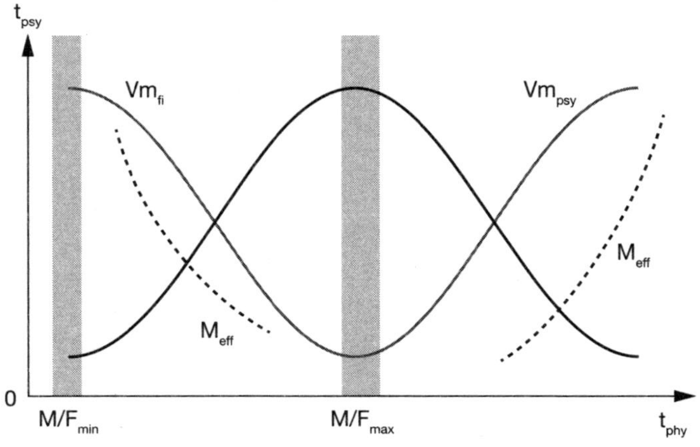

FIGURE 6. *Cycle of velocities of money and temporalities*

CHAPTER 2

Weeks 3 & 4
The recomposition of memory patterns

At the starting point (observation t), there are dominant negative patterns which invade *both* the imaginary space R within memory recall *and* the discourse of the participants (war, Spanish flu). We stress the analogy between memory and narrative which, always and throughout, provides the underlying elements of economic and market phenomena.

THE THEORY. PATTERNS, IMAGE-OBJECTS AND NARRATIVES

The theory here is that (i) the crisis creates a split within the referential R, breaking a narrative which has been established on the basis of a high level of forgetting, (ii) a hyper-dominant pattern is installed within the downward trend, (iii) and then makes way for a fragmentation of M with conflicting and opposing patterns, none of which prevails for a certain period of time (consistent with a phase of rebounds and falls in market values), with intersecting narratives of both a positive and negative nature, within a sort of search for reference points within memory, (iv) until a new narrative triumphs with certain dominant patterns once again (whether positive or negative).

Time sequences of the crisis

Initially, there are two dominant patterns (image-objects) of a past war and pandemic, forming the initial structure (io_1, io_2), which generally, if not completely, occupy the psychological referential R. They correspond to negative narratives, in the sense that they include memorised elements which may lead to a decrease in values – specifically on the markets, here.

This disruptive sequence of forgetting is also that of a disruption of the real and financial velocities.

We stress the notion of a *narrative* (of memory or of language) since, as it were, once the sequence of forgetting is disrupted, a path for the recomposition of memory opens up, which must lead to the constitution of another narrative.

In t_3, coming up to mid-April, image-objects other than those which formed the initial structure (io_1, io_2) can be seen moving through the narratives. Some of these are more positive (the observation of the second derivatives of the virus cycle with a few early signs of deceleration; a rise in Chinese manufacturing figures for the first time; new actions from the monetary and budgetary authorities, particularly in the USA).

This t_3/t_4 sequence shows conflicts between image-objects and a more fragmented and more manifold enrichment of the referential R since the initial pattern (io_1, io_2).

This represents a pattern of rises in values, which are not, most of the time, sustainable. What we call volatility is consistent with this sequence of the referential R of a (re)composition of memory.

Accordingly, what is predominantly recalled after the image-objects which have determined the disruption of forgetting (io_1, io_2), is, on observation, a series of manifestations of the initial pattern (io_1, io_2), with what is now a relatively positive bias. This is true of the monitoring of the accelerations or decelerations of numerous series linked to the virus cycle. The appropriation and gradual control of (io_1, io_2) by the actors is reflected by the setting of standards for the two image-objects, which allows for a possible interpretation (whether true or false) and this, of itself, maintains a connection with the emotions.

This leads to a return of the more positive io. Rather than the io of projection and vision (day after), which are symmetrical to the visions of past wars and pandemics, these are more a memory of forms and structures which show how such events are usually, and over and beyond their immediate, unusual and exceptional aspect, located within time and space, in forms which always mark a (cyclical) end to the event or to the opposing forces. The narratives of this sequence are clearly directed towards the question of the duration of that which is happening, that of the opposing forces (with significant uncertainties, given the lack of any treatment for the virus).

Memory is confronted by a dual event: with both health and economic-financial aspects. The phase of memory recall therefore witnesses image-objects which are seeking to attach themselves to these two channels, with links within R (they are both consistent with the form of a wave, and analogies within the imaginary world combine the two components).

The attempt to place the event within, as it were, a standardised, interpretative framework characterises the t_3/t_4 sequence. Within this sequence, memory is both that which drives the correction, at first in a very emotional manner, based on pure image-objects as images (images of the June 1940 exodus, those coming from old documentaries on the Spanish flu, a narrative of the great plagues which all came from Asia…), and then in a more standardised manner, where the memory proposes limits or norms (a pandemic finally comes to an end, it undergoes a cycle, the contraction of activity is temporary in nature, there are examples within the past…) and, therefore, also seeks to show the limits and provide a framework for the pandemic sequence.

Based on this, although it is still too early to say at this point in time (writing in real time),

(i) we can posit that M will ultimately attract positive image-objects,

(ii) while the rate of forgetting of the initial patterns will increase,

(iii) the exit pattern would combine a positive memory and the forgetting of the event within its initial manifestations of memory.

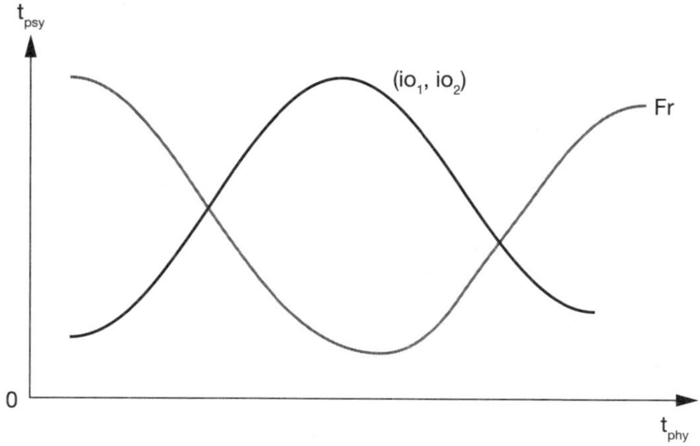

FIGURE 7. *Rate of forgetting and initial patterns of the image-objects*

A READING OF THE CRISIS

The coronavirus offers a situation, where one can observe:

- uncertainty (the virus was not improbable but, once it occurred, we realise that this virus was not expected, that avenues for treatment or a vaccine are not provided for);

- the relationship with time, the lengthening of physical time, which is, as it were, objective and linked to the lockdown sequences, which will be followed by the exiting sequences out of lockdown, but also and above all distortions of psychological time with contractions and dilations. In particular, we try to pay attention to the specific, observable manifestations of these dilations or contractions.

Psychological velocity of money as circulation of the image-objects per monetary unit

The initial shock (an exponential rise in the number of persons contaminated by the virus or who have died as a result thereof; the collapse of the financial markets and of certain sectors of economic activity) seems to correspond to a contraction of psychological time linked to an acceleration in the circulation of image-objects (io) within the referential R. The psychological velocity is the circulation of the io.

$$V_{psy} = V_{io}$$

The psychological velocity of money corresponds to the circulation of the image-objects per monetary unit ($Vm_{psy} = Vm_{io}$).

Accordingly, psychological time experiences an initial contraction phase, where everything seems to take place more quickly, albeit within a physical time referential which, in turn, gradually slows down or freezes.

In a later phase, the distancing of the physical horizons (the exiting lockdown or treatment, for the virus; the recovery of the markets or revival of business, for the economy) and the very physical reality of lockdown (confinement, desocialisation…) seem to be able to produce a stretching of the psychological time-matter. Entering a dilation phase of psychological time would correspond to an acceleration of V_{io} within the referential R.

NARRATIVES AND THE CIRCULATION OF IMAGE-OBJECTS IN THE PSYCHOLOGICAL REFERENTIAL

The practical link between the phenomena of the psychological referential R (memory, forgetting, internal temporality of the consciousness or psychological temporality), which we have described and, second, the existence of the narratives, within the sphere of language, which accompany these phenomena of the referential R within the execution of the economic and financial facts, constitutes a striking fact of observation in respect of the Covid-19 crisis.

Based on the striking analogy between the structure of the discourse of R and the narrative which accompanies any economic or financial phenomenon, empirical material can be gathered which provides support, by way of observation, to our more theoretical descriptions.

We thus add to the dimensions followed in the Covid crisis, that of the narrative and the discourse, for which we posit that, in empirical terms, it is a physical field which is accessible for observation, where the image-objects of R are attached; here, for example, the initial images in memory recall of past wars and pandemics. Moreover, this narrative retroacts or acts upon R, which is understood as a discourse itself.

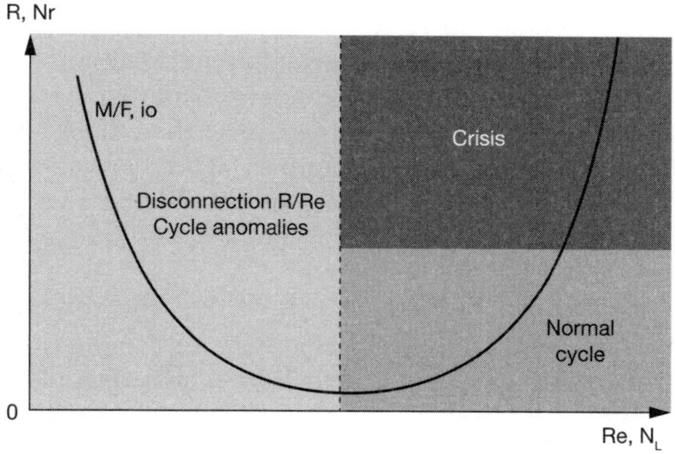

FIGURE 8. *Representation of the cycle*

We are, therefore, describing two narratives, N_R (the structure of the psychological referential as a discourse) and N_L (the structure of language, which is observed within the physical description of the economic and financial phenomena), in respect of which we know that only N_L is observable but in respect of we can posit an analogy or proximity with N_R and, consequently, rely upon that analogy in order to obtain an empirical description of N_R and, consequently, of R.

We can formulate a hypothesis that the means of investigation made available by big data, by artificial intelligence (AI) and other types of machine-learning are now able to detect, identify and standardise the patterns of memory and their dynamic of dominance and of forgetting, the structures combining the image-objects and networks by means of which they form impacting narratives. Mere analysis of the occurrences does not suffice, the dynamics are even more important, as is the velocity of the image-objects. We must, therefore, be able to identify a few forms of the speed of circulation of image-objects within the *real* sphere or referential which is, therefore, observable ($V_{io(Re)}$). Ultimately, it becomes possible to construct a mapping of the referential R through analysis of the real film which is superimposed upon it, within and through the narrative which fully constitutes the economic and financial phenomenon.

The Covid crisis has made it possible to detect, in particular because they have suddenly emerged as if from nowhere, image-objects which have come from far away, pandemic and warlike memory patterns whose counterparts, in a form of analogon, are the numerous recurrences and incidences of evocation within the discourse produced during the crisis. These image-objects, as we have, moreover, described them, a production of consciousness as an imaginary world, as analogons of reality or pure illusion, have taken on these latter two forms in the crisis, the cinematographic references providing both the references and the mirror effects.

The circulation of image-objects within the psychological referential (t_{psy}) cannot be confused with that of the (io) within the real referential (t_{phy}) – which have a different nature and temporality – even if, in fact, the memory patterns which circulate within reality are related to the image-objects which structure them.

UPDATE. PRINCIPAL HYPOTHESES

At this stage, we can clarify matters as follows:

(a) We have described the irruption of the crisis as an increase in psychological time, in the sense that there is an acceleration/rise in movement within the referential R, *i.e.* in the circulation of the image-objects io, directed by a dominant phenomenon of memory recall after a top-of-the-cycle phase which was characterised by a high rate of forgetting. The memory recall phase has been described as a phase where psychological time contracts ($t_{psy} = f(V_{io})$) – the acceleration of io facilitates the contraction of the time of perception.

(b) This follows a top of the cycle invaded by forgetting, with a decline in t_{psy} (in the sense of a low speed of circulation of the io) and a dilation of perceived time. The dilation of perceived time is inversely proportional to the speed of circulation of the image-objects within the psychological referential, and is proportional to the rate of forgetting.

We have thus posited that ΔM, *i.e.* the memory recall, was linked to an increase in the velocity of circulation of the image-objects within the referential (V_{io}, R) and a contraction, a shortening of perceived time (t_{psy}), and, consequently, to a psychological velocity of money, *i.e.* the movement of image-objects (their speed of circulation) per unit of monetary account, which increases for velocities of money within the real and financial spheres which are, for their part, reduced. Symmetrically, we have posited that ΔF, *i.e.* the act of forgetting, was linked to what is meant by forgetting (F) and the rate of forgetting (Fr), *i.e.* a slowdown in the circulation of the image-objects within the referential R (V_{io}, R) and, consequently, a lengthening, an elongation of perceived time (dilation of t_{psy}). All the variables described above are unchanged but take the opposite sign.

We asked whether M and F were, so to speak, unequivocal, *i.e.* kept the same meaning; namely whether ΔM has been linked in the example of the crisis to a negative form of memory recall and, therefore, to the decrease in Vm_{fi}, Vm_{Re} within a reversal of the financial and real cycles; and whether, symmetrically, ΔF has been linked to a maximum value at the top of the cycle which precedes the decrease.

Questions

Various questions arise:

(i) What do we do with, how do we handle the patterns and image-objects (io) of a positive type which systematically appear at a certain stage of the process and on which, presumably, the pattern of the cycle recovery and the real and financial velocities can be based? There would, therefore, be values of ΔM linked to rising values of Vm_{fi} and Vm_{Re} and, equally, positive values of ΔM linked to a fall in Vm_{psy} (the relationship is not changed, *i.e.* between the velocity of the (io) within R and Vm_{psy}, where $V_{io} = f(M)$).

(ii) How, within a theory which hypothesises that it is memory recall (ΔM) which generates the energy of the velocity of circulation within R, do we make ΔM into a variable which is not unequivocal, *i.e.* which plays a positive and negative role within the cycle? By then positing, for example, that the cyclical downturns correspond to (ΔM_{io}), *i.e.* to patterns which are attached to dominant image-objects; we can then make a hypothesis that it may concern negative or positive image-objects; consequently, with these hypotheses, we can describe sequences where ΔM may acquire positive or negative values (ΔM_p, ΔM_n) which are, respectively, linked, to increases (decreases) in the real and financial velocities. The psychological velocity of money is increasing, for its part, in both cases (ΔM_p, ΔM_n), since we have, moreover, made a hypothesis that Vm_{psy} was a function of $(V_{io})_R$ and, therefore, of ΔM, since it is ΔM which is the source of energy, movement and speed within the psychological time referential.

(iii) But what then becomes of ΔF within the rationale of the hypotheses discussed above? Just like ΔM, ΔF could acquire values of a positive or negative quality (we mean by this images which can steer the real or financial cycle in a favourable or unfavourable manner) *i.e.* (ΔF_p, ΔF_n); we are then positing, in symmetry with the reasoning adopted above, that the cyclical downturns correspond to (ΔF_{io}), but here it is not a question of (io), which the process might be attached to (there are no io or at least the rate of forgetting Fr causes them to dissolve up until their disappearance) but rather a question of Fr's action on the io or on the patterns and structures of M; accordingly, at the top of the cycle, ΔF is at its maximum; *i.e.* Δr has eliminated all the (M_{io}), whether positive or negative; the cyclical upswing is described as an increase in Fr; at the bottom of the cycle, ΔF can also be described as being at its maximum, since there is a dissolution by Fr of the negative io. ΔF is a rate of forgetting Fr, which is at its maximum at the two extreme points of the cycle, whilst ΔM acquires values of a positive or negative quality at both the top of the cycle and during it.

CHAPTER 3

Week 5
Three hypotheses on the act of forgetting and memory

EVENTS

In t_5, there is an acceleration of a recovery in the price of shares, together with a (lesser) reduction in the bond risk premia. The short-term pattern of asset prices seems to be in sync with the second derivative of a certain number of series, of the cycle of cases infected by the virus, and with the announcements of (supposed) progress in the search for a treatment for the virus. At the same time, uncertainty persists concerning the medium-term outlook, where the anticipations do not seem to be entrenched, due to hesitations concerning the temporary or permanent nature of the real shock, which itself depends upon a certain number of variables which are correlated with the feedback loop (monetary and budgetary actions, risks linked to liquidity and solvency, time function...). There seems to be a very short-term M/F_{ST} pattern and a longer-term $(M/F)_{LT}$ pattern.

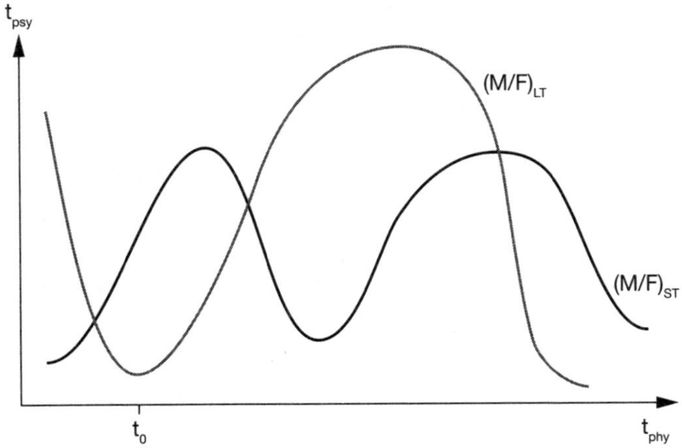

FIGURE 9. *The short-term and long-term (M/F) patterns*

A certain type of short-term event, although not all events, is likely to influence the trajectory of longer-term anticipations. This does not prevent certain events from producing effects over the short-term, whether or not linked to the essential components of the trajectory of $(M/F)_{LT}$ (accordingly, if $(M/F)_{LT}$ is directed by image-objects from former pandemics without any treatment, then $(M/F)_{ST}$ will have an even greater reaction to any announcements concerning such treatments; this seems to be the case in t_5 with the CIVEAD laboratory which has raised early hopes). Although, in t_5, it would still not be possible to redirect $(M/F)_{LT}$, which is still negative in its contribution to the longer-term anticipations.

It therefore seems that, in t_5, we remain within the framework:

- of a psychological temporality of contraction ($M/F\uparrow$) of R with an increase in the speed of circulation within the psychological referential R (*i.e.* $Vm_{psy} \nearrow$);
- but with the appearance of a short-term cycle.

This situation can be described either by distinguishing between $(M/F)_{ST}$ and $(M/F)_{LT}$ or by maintaining the idea of there being only one (M/F) which would consequently experience, within an unchanged trajectory, a short-term dip, *i.e.* a deceleration (second derivative).

THE RATE OF MEMORY RECALL (Mr)

The economists, e.g. Simon or Allais, have essentially, if not completely, tended to consider the rate of forgetting (unlike someone like Bergson who, for his part, tended not to consider forgetting at all and to discuss only memory). In all our works, we have posited:

- the need to take into consideration *both* the Mr and Fr dimensions;
- admittedly, the mirror effect in play between Mr and Fr, but also the access given by each of the two variables to a specific dimension;
- accordingly, the acts of remembering and forgetting constitute acts of consciousness and perception which we distinguish between. One does not remember in exactly the same way one forgets and we advance the asymmetrical or dissymmetrical features as between forgetting and memory.

The act of forgetting and memory

Forgetting (F), in the description which we put forward, corresponds to a dilation of R and of t_{psy} within R. Memory corresponds to a contraction of R and of t_{psy} within R. To be even more precise:

- it is the act of forgetting (*i.e.* the rate of forgetting Fr) and the memory recall (*i.e.* the rate of memorisation or rate of memory recall Mr) which correspond to the phenomena of dilation and contraction of R;
- it is the speed of circulation within R which characterises the phenomena of dilation and contraction of R.

Forgetting and memory are thus described as speeds, as vectors of speed within the psychological referential R. The rate of forgetting or of the act of forgetting Fr, together with the rate of memorisation or of memory recall, correspond to phenomena of acceleration and deceleration, and therefore to V_R for the speed of displacement within the referential R, and thus to second derivatives of M and F ($\Delta_{M/F}$). Forgetting and memory are in fact, in this instance, described as acts of the design of consciousness and perception: M and F only appear (only exist) through Mr and Fr.

Memory recall of patterns of past wars or pandemics

When we observe the memory recall of patterns of past wars or pandemics:

- there is an increase in the speed of displacement within R *i.e.* V_R;
- there is a perception of an acceleration in physical time, which may, moreover, correspond to a reality of t_{phy}. Accordingly, the first phase of the decrease, which will form the essential part of the final, total decrease, as noted in the great majority of significant corrections, is carried out within a very rapid period of time t_{phy}, whose counterpart is a contraction of R with an increase in the speeds of displacement V_R and of Mr.

The nature of forgetting. Forgetting is an acceleration

But then why not also describe the act of forgetting itself as an acceleration, in the sense that forgetting is an effort or act of design, just like memory recall? We could say that we forget more or less quickly or intensely. But the act of forgetting is not of the same nature as that of memory. Forgetting cancels, deletes, casts aside, extracts from the consciousness (of) – forgetting cancels or rather suspends the act of consciousness, while at the same time being the product itself of a design of consciousness and, therefore, of an act of consciousness. This act does not target anything, it even targets nothingness, a pure obliteration of that which is or of that which is recalled. Memory, in turn, targets and constitutes an image, whether or not based on existing patterns. Forgetting does not target or create any images, it does not target anything, its temporality is suspension, its design is obliterating, since that which is forgotten is in the mode of non-being, whilst that which is recalled is equipped with a more substantial mode of being.

Be that as it may, there is indeed a speed of forgetting, whose analogon is a perceived temporality of a more or less rapid flow of forgetting. Can we state that forgetting is the psychological temporality of the dilation of the Subject's psychological referential (the dilation is then based on the hypothesis that, since the act of forgetting does not mobilise or create any image-objects, it involves little or no displacement within R and, therefore, its psychological temporality does not undergo the acceleration which is specific to the displacement within R) and then also state that, in certain circumstances, we can forget quickly (it is more likely that this concerns the perception of the time of forgetting within the physical referential)? We must reflect, without contradiction, upon the fact that forgetting is an elongation of R and of the psychological temporality and, at the same time, that this dilation can be perceived as arriving quickly.

By hypothesis, the obliteration within R in the act of forgetting corresponds to a dilation of t_{psy}. The internal time of consciousness is lengthened within the act of suspension of the image-objects.

Forgetting is a deceleration of V_R, which is itself more or less rapid. Memory is an acceleration of V_R, which is more or less fast-paced.

THE TRIPLE HYPOTHESIS ON MEMORY RECALL AND THE ACT OF FORGETTING. H1, H2, H3

The act of forgetting (the rate of forgetting Fr) and the memory recall (the rate of memorisation Mr) are vectors of V_R.

$$(Mr, Fr) = f\,(V_R)$$

We have stated that (i) we move within R in the same way that we remember or forget. We have also posited (ii) the hypothesis that we anticipated in the same way that we remembered or forgot. And we have also stated that (iii) we moved more or less quickly, the more intensely we remembered or forgot. These hypotheses have been advanced in our works (see *Money, Memory and Asset Prices; Essays in Positive Investment Management*; *The Economic and Financial Order*). Let us compare them with the lines of argument that we have just advanced.

(i) This first hypothesis (H1) is not in contradiction, since we have posited that Mr and Fr were functions of V_R, where Mr is a positive, increasing, non-linear function of V_R and Fr a negative, decreasing, non-linear function of V_R.

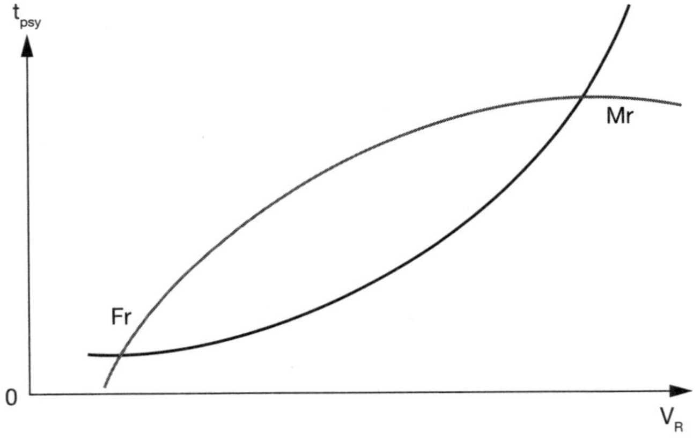

FIGURE 10. *The rate of memory recall and of forgetting in the psychological referential*

(ii) This second hypothesis (H2), which clarifies H1, and which describes V_R, according to the intensity of memory and forgetting, is also not in contradiction but merits further explanation. To forget or to remember more intensely or strongly corresponds to the direction and level of Mr and Fr. The more intense the memory recall, the higher the level of Mr and the more it increases. The more intense the act of forgetting, the higher the level of Fr and the more it increases.

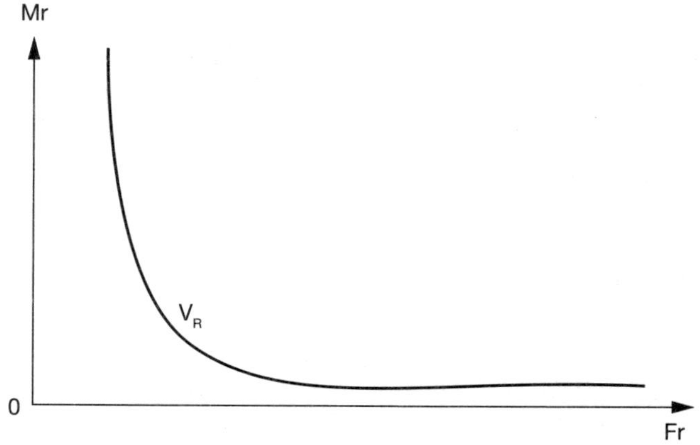

FIGURE 11. *Rate of memory recall, rate of forgetting and velocity within the psychological referential*

(iii) Nor does the third hypothesis (H3), which incorporates the future and the formation of anticipations, contradict our lines of reasoning, insofar as we posited, in our earlier works, that the notion of future is artificial (stemming from a spatial distinction and from physical clock-time, where duration and psychological time or the internal time of consciousness prevail); consequently, we have a formation of anticipations based on the passage of duration as a raw material which removes the spatial distinctions of temporality, and based on consciousness as perception and memory whose internal temporality is provided by the memory recall and the act of forgetting. To anticipate means to project oneself through consciousness–perception (consciousness–perception is ahead of itself) by recalling, which has the specific meaning of the design and construction of image-objects (and their combinations). As such, to anticipate is to remember as an internal act of consciousness.

And so, what about forgetting? In what sense can we say that to anticipate is also to forget? We can first state that any act of design of memory is a design *of* something, and we have posited that this design is a constitution of image-objects through the obliterating design of the external object from the real world: the design of memory targets in order to create being in the mode of non-being, the activation of a function of an imaginary world which we have described (see the second part of *La dynamique boursière*). The design may also be understood as a reminder of image-objects which are created, whether individually or in a group. Consequently, we can also say that any design of memory must, in order to attain that which it wants to remember, identify, create or construct, choose *not to* remember, identify, create or construct infinite numbers of possible image-objects or combinations thereof: the design of memory can only attain its goal by forgetting that which it does not target, that which it does not choose. The function of forgetting is, as such, involved in a game of mirrors with the function of memory.

The function of forgetting suspends that which is not targeted by the function of memory, it is that which excludes from the field and temporality of the design of consciousness. The act of suspension (we use the term "suspension", since the status of that which is struck by forgetting is not final) is a suspension of the internal temporality, which we have compared to an elongation or dilation.

Moreover, the function of forgetting can be seen as an obliterating force. Accordingly, given that to anticipate is to target, it is also to forget, since the design of memory is an act of forgetting. Where there is memory, there is also forgetting. It seems, however, that there exist configurations where, as it were, the function of forgetting is empowered, transcends and completely invades the internal consciousness – this point where everything seems to have been forgotten seems to correspond to the extreme situations of bubbles, of hyperinflation, but also of depression or deflation, since the function of forgetting, which suspends, may suspend positive image-objects as well as negative ones.

The anticipation structure is thus based on forgetting and we also anticipate in the same way that we forget.

Overall, the hypotheses H1, H2, H3 are adopted throughout the whole of our reasoning and our description.

CHAPTER 4

Week 6
The superimposition of physical time and psychological time

EVENTS

We are in t_6. The general context remains that of a perception of appeasement which is levelling off. The temporal sequences (t_{phy}) are:

- the shock of the virus (t_0)
- the shock to the financial markets (t_a)
- the counter-shock policy mix (t_b)
- the stabilisation of the financial markets (counter-shock?) (t_c)
- the real shock (t_d).

UNDERSTANDING SEQUENCE I OF THE CRISIS.
THE SUPERIMPOSITION OF SI (t_{phy}) AND OF SI (t_{psy})

These five elements form what seems to be a loop sequence I. The elements seem to follow one another within physical time; in fact, the majority continue to be superimposed on a persistent basis, like an echo of the impact or the influence, like a resonance. Still, in terms of perception, there is a paradoxical segmentation since, for example, the real shock of this first sequence (SI) comes at the end of SI, when the markets have stabilised or have even rebounded.

We posit that SI = f (t_a, t_b, t_c, t_d, t_e … t_n).

We remark that the financial markets variable is the subject of two observations. SI is observed within a referential of physical time t_{phy}. Therefore, we record the sequence as SI (t_{phy}).

We posit the hypothesis that a sequence exists within the psychological referential, whether in parallel or superimposed, which is recorded as SI (t_{psy}). This sequence incorporates the elements structured by memory, forgetting and duration and its image-object is the elementary reference (io). The temporal sequences of R (t_{psy}) are:

- the zero image-objects $(io)_0$; in this instance, these are images of past pandemics or wars whose presence we have described. We make the hypothesis that, in any S sequence, there are one or more primary patterns or primary image-objects which, just like the patient zero in medicine, will play a role in the viral dissemination dynamic – we make express recourse to the analogy between the dissemination of a virus and the dissemination of the dynamic and the energy within SI, particularly since this crisis offers a unique observation study: the analogical reasoning is overtaken by reality, since the physical virus is there, at the same time as its analogon, the virus which circulates within the markets and within the real economy, the physical virus being, in addition, the source of its analogon.

What is specifically viral in the observed sequence? The dynamic which results from the initial patterns $(io)_0$ of memory recall. The virus (analogon) circulates within R in the same way that the image-objects move and which, starting from a patient zero $(io)_0$, will aggregate or combine differentiated forms, which may possibly be more complex.

There is, therefore, a reality of displacement of the $(io)_0$ and a speed (velocity) of such virus analogons (v_a), *i.e.*:

$$(V(io)_0)_R$$

- the second generation image-objects $(io)_1$ stemming from what we have called the recomposition process of memory patterns, namely, starting from $(io)_0$, in an ever more complex tree structure, an ordered but very possibly conflicting multiplication, of (io) and combinations thereof in aggregate forms; the associated (and not simply analogical) counterpart of this phase, which resembles the drawing up of a language, is the construction of narratives within the physical referential;

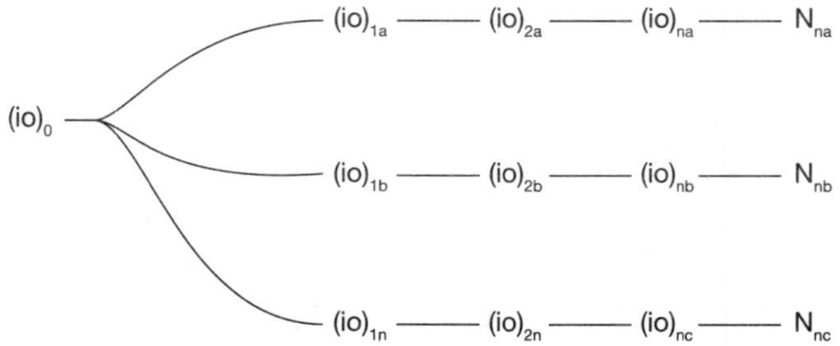

FIGURE 12. *Structure of the image-objects and narratives*

- the narratives (N_1, N_2... N_n) appear at the end of the creative iterations of subdivisions and complexifications of the so-called second (n) generation image-objects described above. These narratives are themselves image-objects, as a structure (see table above). Symmetrical to these are the narratives which, in the physical world, traverse the markets and the real economy.

We henceforth have two structures, SI (t_{phy}) and SI (t_{psy}), which provide an understanding of the whole of the first sequence of the Covid crisis, which we have described.

THREE-DIMENSIONAL TABLE. THE HORIZONTAL, VERTICAL AND DIAGONAL GENOMIC CHAINS

	$(io)_0$			
t_0				
	$(io)_{1a}$	$(io)_{2a}$	$(io)_{3a}$	$Na_{(HGC)}$
t_a				
	$(io)_{1b}$	$(io)_{2b}$	$(io)_{3b}$	N_b
t_b				
	$(io)_{1c}$	$(io)_{2c}$	$(io)_{3c}$	N_c
t_c				
	$(io)_{1d}$	$(io)_{2d}$	$(io)_{3d}$	N_d
t_d				
	$N_{1(VGC)}$	N_2	N_3	N_4

FIGURE 13. *Representation of the image-objects and narratives within physical time*

We construct a simple table which presents the two dimensions SI (t_{phy}) and SI (t_{psy}). We allocate to each sequence of physical time (real referential R_e) a genomic series or bundle made up, first, on a direct horizontal line, of the image-object or image-objects which appear within the complexification process $(io)_0$, and the memory recomposition process (which we have called second generation). We briefly describe the characteristics of the physical, temporal sequence and the $(io)_{na}$ which dominate the sequence. For example, for t_b, a sequence of physical time within the real referential, we identify image-objects $(io)_{1a}$, $(io)_{2a}$ and $(io)_{3a}$ which structure the sequence within psychological time (referential R):

- the image-objects have a unitary and autonomous character, in the sense that they are new patterns and images which are recalled and seem different from $(io)_0$ (accordingly, $(io)_0$ is made up of image-objects of past pandemics and wars, for the unexpected, physical, temporal sequences $(t_a, t_b)t$, whilst within sequences t_c or t_d, (io) appear with a more positive memory);
- the same is true of the memorised action patterns of the central banks in 2008, which may cancel a more negative genomic series, where the central bank action was either absent or ineffective (Fed, 1929 crisis; Japan in the 1990's). Accordingly, $(io)_{1a}$ may be interpreted individually, in the sense that it is characterised by a specific core (e.g., Fed 1929);
- that said, the $(io)_n$ are linked (they form a genomic chain which is consistent with our hypothesis H1, of which heredity constitutes a major dimension) and, therefore, we make the hypothesis that they are dependent on each other, and all on $(io)_0$. Accordingly, for t_x (t_{phy}), where $n \geq 1$, we have:

$$(io)_{nx} = f\left((io)_{n-1}, x, (io)_0\right) (t_{psy})$$

(i) A horizontal reading of the table thus gives a first dimension, that of the *horizontal genomic chain* (HGC), *i.e.* the genomic sequence (*i.e.* the structure of the image-objects within the psychological referential) which corresponds to a given sequence of the referential within physical time. This chain leads to a specific narrative N_n. The narrative is a function of the elements of the genomic chain, *i.e.*:

$$N_n = f\left((io)_{nx}\right) (t_{psy})$$

(ii) A vertical reading of the table gives a second dimension, that of the *vertical genomic chain* (VGC), *i.e.* the sequence of the structures of image-objects within the psychological referential which corresponds to *the whole* of the sequences of the real referential within physical time.

Accordingly, for t (t_{phy}), taking y values for each temporal sequence, *i.e.* $y_a, y_b \ldots y_n$ and, therefore, for ty (t_{phy}), we have:

$$(io)_{ny} = f\left((io)_{n,}\ y_n–y_{n-1,}\ (io)_0\right) (t_{psy})$$

This chain leads to a specific narrative $N_{n'}$. The narrative is a function of the elements of the genomic chain (VGC), *i.e.*:

$$N_{n'} = f\left((io)_{ny}\right) (t_{psy})$$

(iii) A diagonal reading of the table gives a third dimension, that of the *diagonal genomic chain* (DGC), *i.e.* the chain of structures of image-objects which combine temporal sequences and structures of the psychological referential, not on the basis of a single sequence of dominant physical time (HGC), nor on the basis of dominant psychological structures of the whole of the real physical sequences at any given moment (VGC), but rather on the basis of a-chronological combinations of the image-objects within the psychological referential, illustrating the property which we ascribe to it of freeing itself from any physical chronology within the constitution of the images and their displacement.

Accordingly, as a method, we construct a matrix for the whole of the sequence SI within the two referentials R and R_e.

WEEK 6 CONTINUED. PATTERNS OF THE DAY AFTER

In sequence t_6, we can see the formation and appearance of image-objects and patterns of the "The Day After" type, which also correspond to literary narratives, stories and which start to *circulate* (we have stressed the importance of the speed of circulation of the (io), *i.e.* $V_{(io)}$) within the economy and on the markets.

These (io) are of interest, since they are the first, since the start of the crisis to present a pure future structure without any apparent or explicit reference to the past, insofar as they do not present themselves as belonging to a memory recall but rather as a pure projection towards the future. They are structured as narratives, presenting themselves as a breach with any past reference or, more often, as an accentuation or extension of pre-existing trends. This is true of deglobalisation (and, in this regard, of the underlying stories, concerning the necessary truncation of the value chains, in particular for reasons of sovereignty), of the issue of inequalities, of the digital capitalism which has emerged stronger as a result of working from home during the crisis. The projection is, however, accompanied by a search for memory patterns as points of reference: accordingly, the 1930's or the 1970's.

Narratives from Eden

What is striking within the initial construction and dissemination of these (io) and patterns, mostly in and through the media, is their positive, benevolent and naive character, in the sense that it is a gentler world which is described, a socio-environmental Eden of positive proximity, without any real limits in terms of finance or policies, a gentle, green and collective regression towards the nostalgia of former times.

It is clear that there are both image-objects which, in our description, we characterise as *illusions* (pure obliterations of reality which are not replaced or structured by (io) which correspond to memory recalls of actual experiences but rather of pure illusory imaginary worlds); but there are also (io) which attach themselves to actual references, such as the 1930's.

The narrative of the "day after", of the "new world", of the "change in regime" triggers in fact a new sequence within the psychological referential (t_{psy}), which corresponds within the real referential to a new temporal sequence (t_{phy}). Let us call this sequence, which commences in temporal sequence t_6, SII. SII (t_{phy}) corresponds to the resurfacing, accordingly with a time delay, of the consequences of the initial shock within the real economy (t_1, t_2 for the references to individual weeks since the very beginning of the crisis; – see Figure 2; t_0 and t_a for the two temporal sequences within physical time which we have characterised – see Figure 13). We are, therefore, talking about sequences where that which is observed or is observable, takes place with a time delay of almost four sequences as compared to the contemporary temporality from which it originates, whether the sequence is defined in terms of time (the week *i.e.* the time span [t_0, t_1, t_2] / [t_6] – see Figure 2) or thematically, *i.e.* the gap/span [t_0 - t_a] / [t_d] – see Figure 13.

Delayed reality

At the same time, SII (t_{psy}) corresponds to the projection towards what we have called a pure future. We can, therefore, observe:

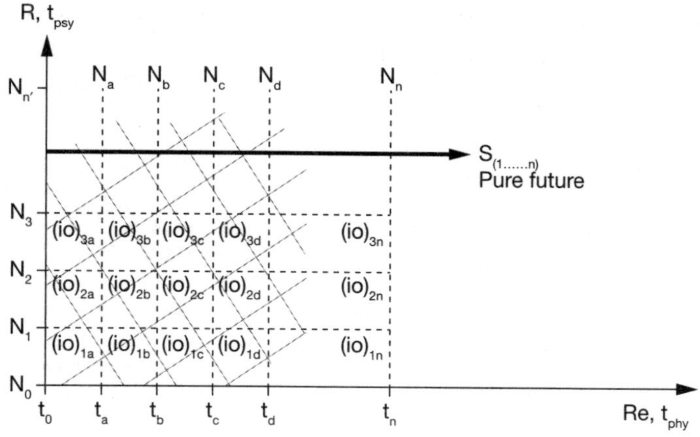

FIGURE 14. *The HGC, VGC and DGC genomic chains*

Simultaneously, within the real referential, there is a very actual reality of the economic shock, the reality of which is not to be denied but, on the contrary, is to be noted, as it were, as appearing now but as, in a certain manner, having already taken place.

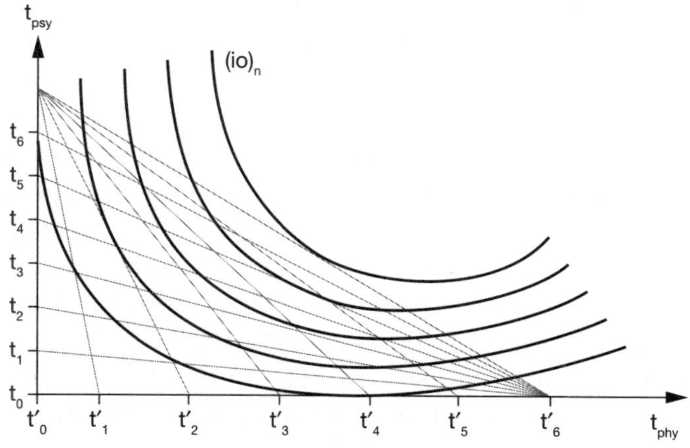

FIGURE 15. *Image-objects and temporal referentials*

That which is observed within the real referential is, systematically, *delayed* or postponed, displaced by a sort of optical effect. And, therefore, the perception of reality is confronted with this delay, which is similar in effect to that of the memory of reality on itself. At the same time, from the viewpoint of the psychological referential, the sequences of (io) create what is observable, *i.e.* the N_n narratives. The psychological time and referential manifest themselves to perception and acquire the status of being observable through the production of narratives, *i.e.* through structures of language which echo the structures of the referential R.

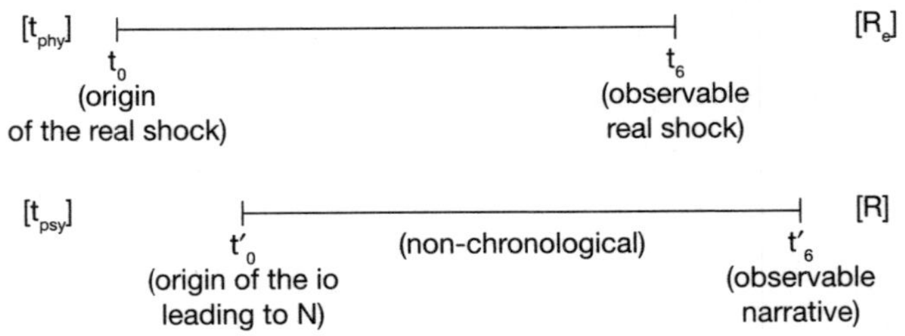

FIGURE 16. *Chronologies of the real and psychological referentials*

Therefore, we only observe two types of elements: (i) real images which come to perception in the same way as the light from distant or former stars; such as the fact, within the crisis, that the shock becomes apparent to perception in t_6 but this is only an image of a shock which occurred in t_0. We are in the real referential and, must not therefore, be misled by the term "image" (it is not the io of the psychological referential); (ii) narratives, stemming from the image-objects of R, which combine the chronology of clocks and thus present two sorts of time difference effects or delay-effects: within the chronological, real referential of physical clock-time, since one narrative follows on from another from the point of view of perception (with, once again, in the same way as for the real facts of an economic shock, which are the delayed image of an original shock, a time gap between the observable narrative at any given moment and its origin, which occurs earlier within clock-time, this anteriority being housed within the io which gave birth to it); but also within psychological time, a confusion of benchmarks and points of reference from clock time, since a prior event may occur later and vice versa.

Questions

In t_6,

- M/F: there is both a forgetting of the initial very negative forms which have been recalled (with a projection towards The Day After) and a recall of historic reference patterns (1930, 1970...). How should we refer to M/F at this stage? What should we call it?

- Vm_{psy}: only forgetting can cause Vm_{psy} to slow down; strictly speaking, there is no forgetting and, on the contrary, memory recalls of image-objects continue to manifest themselves. Or, alternatively, should we consider that the projection which appears in t_6 (The Day After) is based on forgetting (the obliteration of reality)?

CHAPTER 5

Weeks 7 & 8
Uncertainty as a dilation of psychological time

EVENTS

In t_7 and in t_8, we are still in a context of rising stock markets and a reduction in credit risk premia. There is a sense that this is exaggerated. Perceived time changes in the sense that it seems to lengthen, to relax and to expand, in contrast to the initial period of perceived sharp acceleration and contraction. This seems to validate our explanatory diagram of the whole. In particular, the rise in asset prices corresponds to a slowdown in the psychological velocity of money (a smaller increase) and a rise in the velocity of money within the financial sphere.

THE RATE OF FORGETTING OF THE INITIAL STRUCTURE

Does this perception of a time which lengthens or slows down, which is thus only perceived in proportion to the contraction (which is literally one of respiration), correspond to a rise in the rate of forgetting? That would be consistent with the principal hypotheses which we have presented: the initial fall is fundamentally a memory recall anchored to the (io) patterns of negative perception which, as it were, constitute the foundation of the perceptive structure of R which is put in place and unfurls across the whole of the period which we are describing, together with its sequences.

We can then describe an overall structure, where the permanence of the founding image-objects (pandemic and warlike io), of a negative nature (*i.e.* likely to create a downward pressure on the anticipations and variables of the real and financial spheres), does not prevent a certain increase in the rate of forgetting of such initial image-objects, a temporary increase (so long as the overall structure of R is not broken; we formulate a hypothesis that there may, at any moment, be a return to the foundation (io)).

It follows that the evolution of the overall period involves a certain rate of forgetting which affects $(io)_0$, *i.e.* $[(io)_0]_{(M/F)}$ and that the rise in the rate of forgetting of $(io)_0$ must be matched by the recall of other, more positive, (io), without eliminating the initial images. The rate of forgetting is thus estimated by comparison with the *initial* structures of R: the dynamic (M/F) of $(io)_0$ should consequently be monitored in order to understand the development of the whole of the sequence.

The lengthening of perceived time would therefore correspond to (i) the increase in the rate of forgetting of the initial structure $(io)_0$; (ii) a slowdown in the speed of circulation of the (io) within R; (iii) an increase in the rate of memory recall based on the more positive (io); this last hypothesis amounts to saying that, at any time, the rate of forgetting *something* (since there has to be *something* which is forgotten) is analysed as the rate of memory recall *of something (else)*, a description of forgetting and of memory as acts of consciousness (which is, always and throughout, a consciousness *of something*) and that this memory recall (n + 1) is only made possible by the act of forgetting (n).

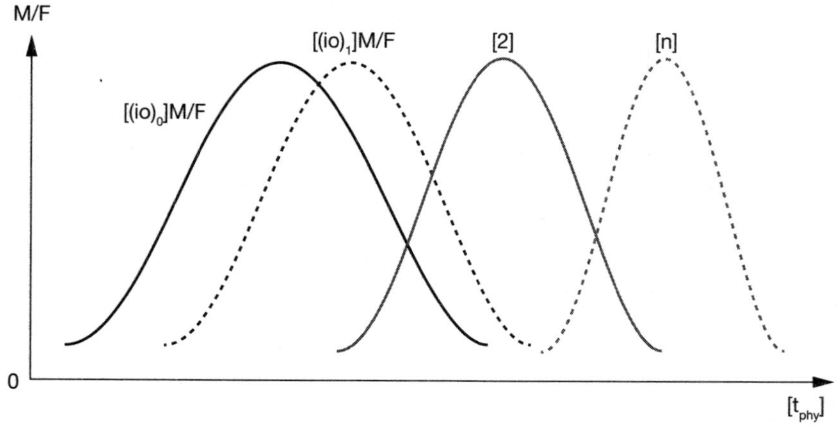

FIGURE 17. *Generation of the cycles of image-objects*

A WAVELIKE STRUCTURE OF VARIATIONS ON THE INITIAL STRUCTURE

A wavelike structure can, therefore, be imagined, where the act of forgetting the initial founding pattern $(io)_0$ would make room, in the manner of waves, for the memory recall of $[(io)_{1,\,2\ldots n}]$ type image-objects, still within the cyclical field of a possible memory recall of $(io)_0$.

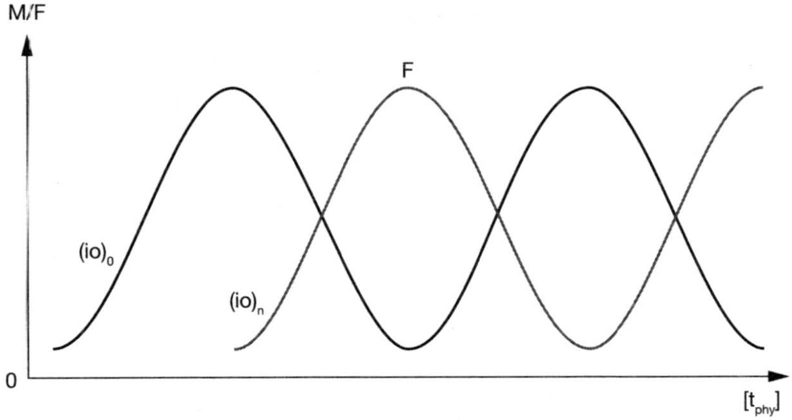

FIGURE 18. *Undulatory waves of image-objects*

$(io)_n$ represents the infinite set of the varying (io) of the initial founding structure $(io)_0$, which themselves have infinite possible cyclical scopes, the essential frequency being provided by $(io)_0$.

Observation of the t_7 sequence and the t_8 sequence and, in particular, of the observable narratives (occurrences of image-objects within the representations and of certain lexical structures within the discourses and language), makes it possible to identify the following points:

(i) the two initial patterns $(io)_0$, the Spanish flu pandemic and the conflict of the second world war, are still present but retreating. Their presence provides a structure, in the sense that they constitute the reference lexical framework for the discourses and narratives. There is, however, a retreat, with less images that are genuinely impressive;

(ii) the pattern of the "day after", which appeared in the previous sequence, is clearly strengthened, which triggers memory recalls referring to recoveries from crisis (the economic context at the end of the second world war; social contexts, in general, at the end of crises, 1945 once more; the end of the Spanish flu). It can thus be seen that (M/F), *i.e.* the memory recall and forgetting dynamic, moves along the memorised, physical, temporal axis (the periods before and after the war or before and after the so-called Spanish pandemic) with, in the sequence, images of a more positive nature. One therefore moves within the psychological referential R *along* a temporal axis of the before and after, which seems to be in line with the chronology of physical time.

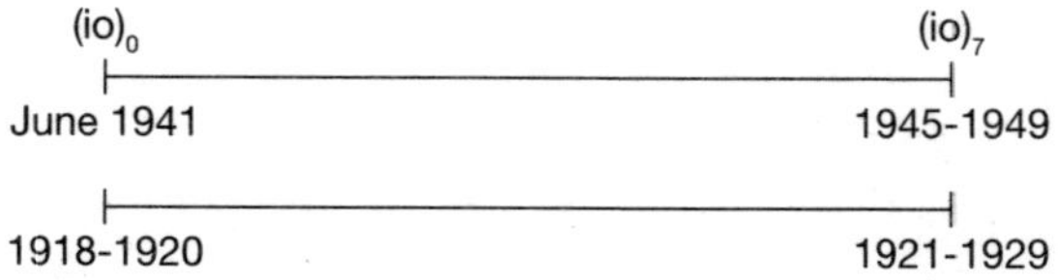

FIGURE 19. *Chronologies of the image-objects*

It can be seen that it is indeed $(io)_0$ which is, as it were, the starting point or the reference point. The sense of an adherence to chronology may be misleading since, at any given time, there may be a return to $(io)_0$;

(iii) perception is dominated by the lengthening of the temporal (physical) horizons, the essential part of the narratives focusing on the fact that "it will be longer". This extension of perceived physical time is a dilation of psychological time. This time passes more slowly. The contrast with, first, the sharp contraction of t_{psy} in the crisis and, second, the projection into an uncertain future contribute to this elongation of time.

UNCERTAINTY TAKES THE FORM OF A DILATION OF PSYCHOLOGICAL TIME

We have Uty (*uncertainty*) and t_{psy}. This is evident within the Covid-19 crisis. This elongation follows, within physical time, upon a sharp contraction of the psychological time of the very first sequences.

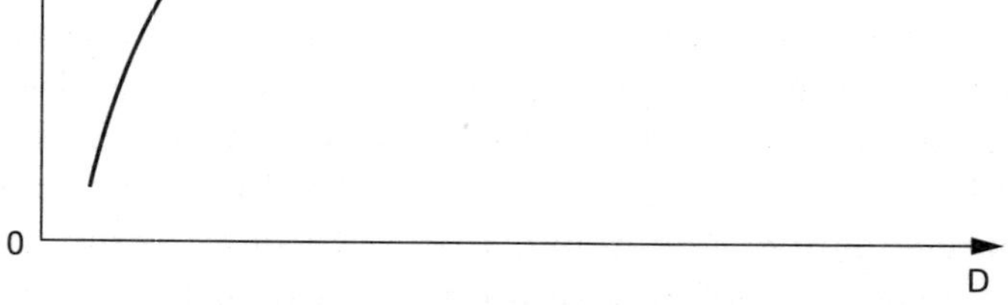

FIGURE 20. *Representation of psychological time. The contraction and dilation functions*

where:
C = contraction
D = dilation

We also have:

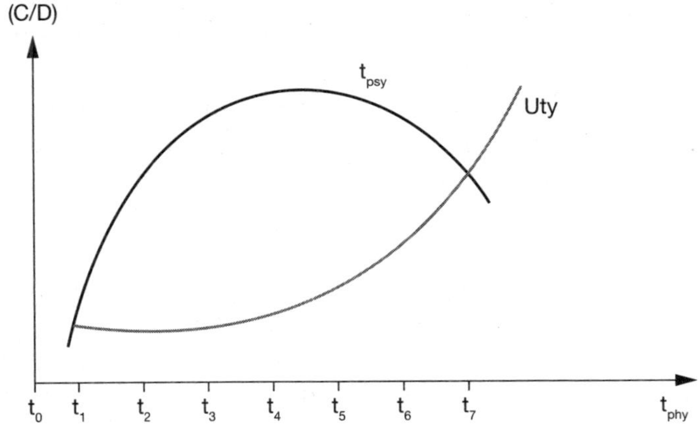

FIGURE 21. *Psychological time and uncertainty*

The (C/D) function

We therefore show:

(i) the (C/D) function which is characteristic of the psychological referential R, which expresses the phenomena of the contraction (C) and dilation (D) of psychological time. The eruption of the crisis coincides with a sharp contraction of psychological time. Accordingly, (C/D) = $f(t_{psy})$;

(ii) (C/D) is a decreasing function of uncertainty in the sense that the uncertainty itself coincides with an increase in the dilation of psychological time. We have (C/D) = f (Uty) t_{psy};

(iii) (C/D) is a function of (M/F), *i.e.* of the function of memory recall and of the act of forgetting. We can observe during the crisis that the eruption of the crisis coincides with a sudden recall (which is also fast-moving within the referential of physical time) of patterns (image-objects (io)) which leads to a first hypothesis (H1).

Testing hypotheses (H1) and (H2). Distortions of psychological time, memory recall or act of forgetting, perceived time and circulation of image-objects in the psychological referential

(H1) The contraction of psychological time coincides with a memory recall. It is accompanied by the phenomena of an acceleration of perceived time (t_{psy}) and an increase in the speed of circulation of the image-objects within R. The acceleration within the referential of psychological time itself coincides with an acceleration within the referential of physical time (the outbreak of the Covid crisis is sudden, quick and takes all players by surprise with incapacitating effects); within this sequence, the contraction of t_{psy} corresponds to an acceleration of the physical phenomena observed within R_e (t_{phy}). We therefore have (C/F), an increasing function of (M/F) *i.e.*:

$$(C/F) = f\,(M/F)\,(t_{psy})$$

(H2) The dilation of psychological time corresponds to an act of forgetting, with phenomena of a deceleration of (t_{psy}) and a reduction in the speed of circulation of the (io) within R. This sequence itself coincides with an increase in uncertainty. Accordingly, by extension of reasoning, the uncertainty would coincide with an increase in the rate of forgetting.

This last hypothesis is far from self-evident and, curiously, one feels more comfortable with (H1) than with (H2), even though it is just its symmetrical image.

(i) Memory recall seems to be more easily linked to movement, to speed, to acceleration and, consequently, to a contraction of perceived time within whose referential the observed phenomena are located. This does not mean, as already discussed, that one cannot be literally struck by forgetfulness, as if suddenly swallowed up in a trap but, as we have emphasised, such a movement does not lead to the creation or displacement of image-objects, but coincides instead with their destruction or slide into lethargy. The movement of memory recall does not make it possible to classify what is recalled as positive or negative: the rate of memory recall (Mr) is neutral from the viewpoint of qualitative analyses, or of qualities.

Accordingly, we can compare the notions of (i) memory recall (and the rate of memory recall Mr which is linked to it) and (ii) the contraction of perceived time within the psychological referential C_R, *i.e.* the function f (Mr, C_R) where C_R = f (Mr).

(ii) It seems more difficult to compare the act of forgetting (and the rate Fr which is linked to it) with the lengthening of perceived time.

A certain number of observations seem to support the connection: at the extreme points of the cycle (such as inflation or a bubble and deflation), a form of suspension can be observed (of the past, of the lessons of history...), an almost infinite form of extension of phenomena (everything seems to be reproduced *in identical form*: there are less and less differences, a spread of uniformity); but also, without this time considering the extreme points of the cycle, when optimism returns after the shock of a crisis, it returns on the basis of an increase in forgetfulness.

FIGURE 22. *Reference patterns*

Questions. The f (Fr, D_R) function

A certain number of questions also arise: how can we assert that the top of the cycle corresponds to a sharp increase in the rate of forgetting, which seems to imply a reference to speed within the psychological referential R (and also within that of physical time, the final periods of bubbles providing a striking example) and, at the same time, assert that the increase in the rate of forgetting corresponds to a slowdown in psychological time and in the circulation of the image-objects within R?

We have associated the speed of displacement within R with the circulation of image-objects. However, the function of forgetting does not create or mobilise such image-objects. Forgetting is a design without image-objects but forgetting is a paradoxical function, as we have already noted, since forgetting is the means by which the design of memory reveals the image-object: we need to forget *everything else* in order for some image-object or other, some pattern or other to present itself to the perceptive consciousness.

Accordingly, the increase in the rate of forgetting within sequence t_7 and sequence t_8, which makes it possible to understand the recovery of the markets when, factually, there are few elements or published information which seem to justify the same,

(i) masks a rotation of image-objects from (negative) $(io)_0$ into (more positive) $(io)_{1, 2...n}$; it is the $(io)_0$ patterns which are struck with a higher rate of forgetting;

(ii) is always the act of forgetting *something*, in this instance $(io)_0$ patterns.

Is it therefore possible to compare the notions of the act of forgetting (and the rate of the act of forgetting Fr which is linked to it) and the dilation of psychological time D, *i.e.* the elongation of perceived time? It seems to us that we can do so, by taking into consideration the remarks made above. Consequently, we must assume, as we indeed do, that the dilation of psychological time, which is an increasing function of forgetting, is a decreasing function of the speed of circulation within the psychological referential R. We are therefore speaking about a function f (Fr, D_R) (where D_R = f (Fr)), as specified.

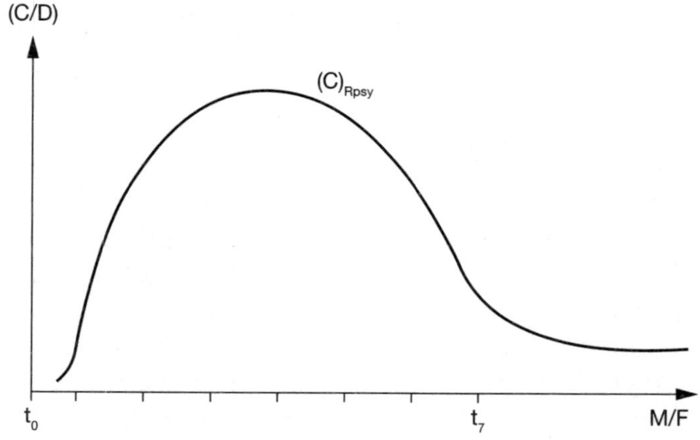

FIGURE 23. *The contraction and dilation functions of psychological time*

The curve $(C)_{Rpsy}$ provides a graphic representation of the functions (C/D) and (M/F) and an estimated position for the sequences between t_n and t_0 on that curve.

CHAPTER 6

Weeks 9 & 10
The real viral forms and their analogons. A simultaneous analogy

Sequence t_8 comes to an end, which seems to consolidate the most recent sequences, with a distancing of market tensions – more within the narratives than in observed reality – which coexists with a depressing narrative concerning the real economy.

In t_9 and in t_{10}, the improvement (or at least apparent improvement) in market conditions and the (actual) increase in asset prices continue to define the situation, whilst the real economy seems to continue to send various negative signals by means of immediate figures and anticipated future declines which invade the narratives.

This leads us to make two types of remark.

(i) As regards financial assets, there is a form of familiarisation with reality *and* with the narratives of stabilisation/rebound. In fact, everything seems to take place as if a few weeks of stabilisation/rebound have produced a habit-forming effect (the *habitus* which we refer to in our works), a short-term memory effect, which seems to conceal the initial, negative patterns and is, therefore, a form of forgetfulness.

This familiarisation, which is, in this instance, optimistic and which produces effects on asset prices, seems to steer attitudes which are detached from the observations and anticipations which can be seen (immediate) or heard (anticipatory narratives), these asset prices seeming, moreover, to incorporate a factor of support from the central banks which is exceptional but which cannot be extrapolated. Are these markets deciphering something which cannot otherwise be observed?

(ii) It is difficult to reconcile the context of market price and reality and the anticipatory narratives of the real economy.

Everything takes place as if, in particular, the narratives, being concerned about the real economy (such narratives being connected to the initial memory patterns from the shock), were dominated by those of the markets, or rather by their behaviour.

One might think that:

(i) there is a conflict between the market patterns and the real economy patterns;
(ii) the real economy patterns remain connected by the (negative) sign to the initial patterns of the crisis – which we will call complete chain or link continuity – *i.e.* an extension of the narrative and the sign;
(iii) what is happening on the markets is either (a) a partial chain or link continuity, which we have described above, *i.e.*, within a homogenous, unitary sequence, the occurrence of a "minor", conflicting deviation (in the sense that, in the vast majority of cases, the initial pattern regains the upper hand, although cases of a "strong" deviation are possible, causing an interruption of the regime and sign), or (b) an interrupted discontinuity, the probability of which is especially high if the sub-sequence of a strong deviation has lasted for a longer period of time.

A TALE OF THREE CYCLES (REAL, FINANCIAL, AND VIRAL)

All the narratives and variables seem to be dominated, as it were, by the pattern of the virus as a cycle.

Within this crisis, there is a coexistence of three cycles, one of which is completely new, that of the virus; in addition, it is (i) as worldwide and international as the cycles of the real economy and as financial assets, (ii) *it offers, for the first time, a remarkable analogy between the phenomenon of real, viral contagion* $(Cv)_{Re}$ *and the phenomenon of contagion within the real and financial spheres i.e.* $(\mathrm{Cv})_{(\mathrm{Sfi},\mathrm{Sre})}$, where Cv is a viral form of contagion; a phenomenon of contagion which can be described as the spread and retreat of a virus within the context of an epidemic.

The cycle of the virus is that of a dissemination/retreat. As are the real cycle and the financial cycle, linked to the phenomena of dilation and contraction within a referential psychological R. Namely $(\mathrm{Cv})_{\mathrm{R}}$.

In both cases, there is a contagion, which includes the momentum of a dissemination (dilation) and a retreat (contraction). There is also a circulation, and words and analogies are important here. The virus circulates in the same way as money within the real and financial spheres or in relation to the psychological referential (the velocities of money Vm_{fi} and $Vm_{R/Re}$; the psychological velocity of money Vm_{psy}).

MONEY AS A PROXY FOR THE VIRUS; THE NOTION OF THE SPEED OF PSYCHOLOGICAL CIRCULATION OF MONEY

We are, therefore, describing a phenomenon of circulation with significant variables, namely the rate of circulation and the remission/recovery rate. More specifically, there exists an analogy between, first, the virus and, second, something of a viral nature which is circulating within the real and financial spheres. The questions are as follows: what, within the real and financial spheres, has to be understood and described as analogous to the virus? Equally, what, within the psychological referential R, must be understood as a virus, or as viral?

(i) Usually, money is the proxy for the virus within the description of velocities and the number of times which it changes hands for the purposes of real and financial transactions.
(ii) We have added another dimension, that of R, with the concept of the speed of psychological circulation of money, *i.e.* the connection which may or may not exist between a given movement of money and the intensity of the displacement within R, which is linked to memory and to forgetting.

However, we do not specifically state what is *viral* within the circulation and contagion despite clearly seeing the striking analogies with the dissemination of a pandemic. There is indeed a dissemination, circulation, acceleration and deceleration

- of money (monetary sphere) within R_e,
- of narratives (sphere of discourse) within R_e,
- of image-objects (io) (sphere of consciousness and of perception) within R.

We have an opportunity to observe the simultaneous dissemination of real viral forms (Covid) and their analogons (within and through the image-objects and narratives).

FROM RATIO (Ct/Rc) (SPEED OF CIRCULATION OF THE VIRUS/RECOVERY RATE) TO RATIO (Ct′/Rc′). THE CONTAGION OF IMAGE-OBJECTS AND RECOVERY RATES IN THE PSYCHOLOGICAL REFERENTIAL

There is contagion (and its Ct rate), and recovery (and its Rc rate - for *recovery*) and, therefore, the ratio (Ct/Rc) which gives us the extent of the epidemic.

We make a hypothesis that the speed of circulation of the image-objects, which structure the narratives, *i.e.* V_R (speed of displacement within the referential R), may, by analogy, be compared to the speed of circulation of the virus (the number of infections for an infected person, which represents the number of transactions for real or financial purposes for a monetary unit, with regard to the definition of the velocity of money within the real and financial spheres).

We have:

Ct = approximation of the speed of circulation of the virus

V_R = speed of circulation of the image-objects within the psychological referential

Vm_{fi} = speed of money within the financial sphere

Vm_{Re} = speed of the circulation of money within the real sphere

Ct/Rc = rate of contagion (speed of circulation of the virus)/recovery rate

What is the analogon of Ct/Rc for the economic and financial phenomena within their respective spheres?

The question concerns Rc in particular. What is the analogical equivalent of a recovery rate, once the contagion is understood as the circulation of image-objects (and the speed thereof) (within the psychological referential) to which memory patterns (within R) and narratives (within R_e, the real referential, that of observed reality) are attached?

The image-object circulates, then withdraws, just like the virus, with an epidemic-style structure (see R. Shiller and his "*narrative economics*").[1] It is the analogon of illness and can be positive or negative. Consequently, the recovery rate can be defined as that which reverses the direction of the image-object,

1. Shiller is inspired by the Kermack-McKendrick SIR Disease Epidemic Model (1927 – Compartmental or SIR Model), where S = fraction of population susceptible; I = infected and now contagious; R = recovered and now immune; S + I + R = 1; c is the contagion parameter and r is the recovery rate.

which is positive or negative in the simplest approach. Accordingly, within the observation of the Covid crisis, it can clearly be seen that there are at first initial image-objects of a negative form (past wars and pandemics), called $(io)_0$, which then make room for the more positive (io).

Thus, in this case:

Ct = contagion (circulation) of the $(io)_0$, where $(io)_0 < 0$, *i.e.* Ct′
Rc = circulation of the $(io)_{1, 2...n}$, where $(io)_{1, 2...n} > (io)_0$, *i.e.* Rc′

(the < and > signs characterising the negativity or positivity of the image-objects in question). There is a recovery, when image-objects appear which present a positive delta (as here) (or negative delta) as compared to the negative $(io)_0$ (as here) (or positive $(io)_0$).

We, therefore, have a ratio of (Ct′/Rc′):

(i) when the memory reference patterns, *i.e.* the initial image-objects $(io)_0$, here the two $(io)_0$ patterns which we identified at the start of the crisis (the Spanish flu pandemic, the reference to war), continue to circulate more quickly than the image-objects $(io)_{1, 2 ... n}$ which present, within the sequences which follow the outbreak of the crisis, an identity which is likely to consider the evolution of the crisis more favourably (while maintaining a link with the initial $(io)_0$, which may re-enter the game at any time) (we have described $(io)_{1, 2...n}$ above: the memorised, positive action of the central banks and governments with a memory recall of positive patterns regarding the treatment of the 2008 crisis), then (Ct′/Rc′) continues to rise and there is, therefore, an increase, circulation or dissemination of the viral analogon, which is $(io)_0$ (with $(io)_0$ being here negative or unfavourable: it could be different if $(io)_0$ is positive). This coincides with an unfavourable market sequence, for the real economy;

(ii) when Rc′ rises faster than Ct′, *i.e.* when the image-objects ($(io)_{1, 2...n}$), which are more favourable here, circulate more or more quickly than the initial unfavourable image-objects $(io)_0$, then (Ct′/Rc′) decreases and there is, therefore, a decrease, withdrawal or contraction of the initial, viral analogon (or, in other words, an increase in the more favourable, analogical, viral forms). This represents a favourable market sequence, for the real economy.

CONTAGION RATES (CIRCULATION) OF ZERO IMAGE-OBJECTS IN RELATION TO IMAGE-OBJECTS WITH A REVERSE POLARITY

The definition of the narratives, their selection or disappearance constitutes, within the real sphere, that of real, observable life, the other side, the analogon and also the extension of the definition, selection or separation of the image-objects within the psychological referential, which is itself tethered to the structures of memory, of forgetting and duration, whose momentum is boosted by memory recall and the act of forgetting.[1]

We thus make the hypothesis that, for a given population, a relative increase in the contagion rates (circulation) of the zero image-objects and those image-objects with a reverse polarity to that of the zero image-objects, steers the zero image-objects within a sequence, which may or may not have an epidemic content within a sequence. Accordingly, in the case of the Covid crisis:

(i) the epidemic on the markets and within the real economy is triggered by the initial $(io)_0$ zero image-objects. In our observation, we have formed a hypothesis of two stylised $(io)_0$ which we have described within the memory recall which houses them: past pandemics, and in particular the Spanish flu; past wars, and in particular the start of the second world war. There is a contagion rate Ct′ for such initial image-objects;

(ii) other image-objects $(io)_{1,\ 2\ \ldots\ n}$ then appear (which may move in the direction of the initial $(io)_0$ or indeed accentuate them, which is not the case here in the observed sequence), observation of which shows that they may temper the initial negativity. There is a contagion rate for these image-objects, which corresponds to the recovery rate for the real virus, *i.e.* the rate of modification of the initial image-objects (improvement or deterioration according to the nature of the initial shock). We have

1. Shiller identifies two lists of narratives. One for the Covid period under review: coronavirus, pandemic, Donald Trump, American Dream, American Greatness, Great Depression, QE, Trade War. Another for "salient" narratives and a broader timeframe: Trump polarisation, strong economy, fake news, great depression, trade war, sustainability, mortgage defaults and indebtedness, new normal and secular stagnation, real estate bubble, digital age.

noted this other contagion rate (the recovery rate) as Rc′ but we could name it the modification rate;

(iii) what we are describing takes place within a *sequence*, *i.e.* the whole of the developments which occur from the emergence of the initial image-objects, with the idea that there is a sequence because the other image-objects which come later $(io)_0$ retain a connection with these initial image-objects. These image-objects $(io)_{1,\,2\,\dots\,n}$, in relation with $(io)_0$ are, as it were, the genes of a DNA, which correspond to what we have called a sequence.[1]

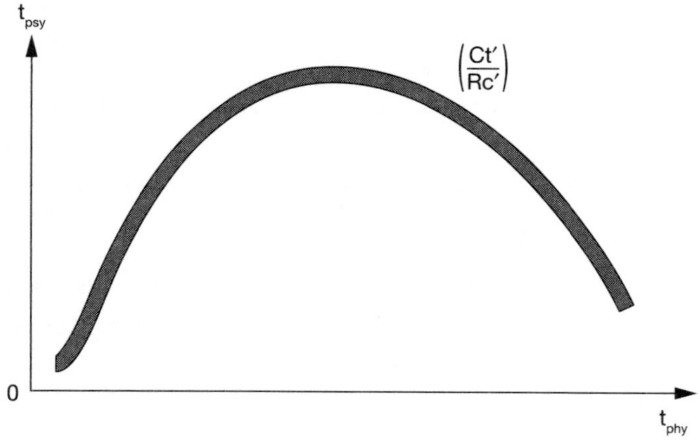

FIGURE 24. *Analogical representation of the rates of contagion and recovery in the temporal referentials*

THE NOTION OF SPEED OF DISSEMINATION. THE COEFFICIENT r′

There is also the question of the speed of transmission or dissemination. A pandemic spreads more or less quickly. This depends upon (i) the contagion rate Ct, *i.e.* the number of people who are newly infected by the infected person (the coefficient r); (ii) the Ct/Rc ratio, *i.e.* the relative trajectory of infections and recoveries.

---

1. With a slightly different definition of the time period under review, Shiller identifies four sequences: A – Pre-crisis; 20 January before the World Health Organisation declares Covid as "a public health emergency of international concern" (30 January); B – Covid expansion; 30 January to 19 February, expansion in the midst of the initial information about the coronavirus crisis; C – Crash; record high in real terms on 19 February – market bottom reached on 23 March; D – V-shaped recovery; 23 March to the present day (September 2020).

This corresponds in our analogical analysis (Ct′) to the rate of occurrence of the zero image-objects $(io)_0$ and, more specifically, to the occurrences within $(io)_{1,\,2\,\ldots\,n}$ which are in the same direction as $(io)_0$, *i.e.* the equivalent of the coefficient r, which we will note as r′. r′ corresponds to the number of image-objects which appear (as *references*, which can be measured by relevant occurrences, *i.e.* those which are likely to produce or to evidence an impact (*spreading*)), which can be considered to be of the same type as $(io)_0$, *i.e.* those which extend their universe, message or approach. The digitalisation of texts and big data/AI should, once again, open up a significant objectivation space.

Therefore, by way of example, for $(io)_{1,\,2\,\ldots\,n} = x(io)_0$; if, for $(io)_0$, we have two initial reference image-objects (our observation and hypothesis in the Covid crisis) and we observe during a second temporal sequence (t_0, t_1, t_2... t_n), *i.e.* the sequence t_1, that there are four reference image-objects which extend the $(io)_0$, then we have $(io)_0 = 2\ (io)_1$, where x = 2; x is the coefficient r′.

This same reasoning is maintained at t = 2 as compared to t_0 and so on; it can also be maintained as between t_n and t_{n-1}.

We therefore have two important variables:

Ct′/Rc′ ; r′

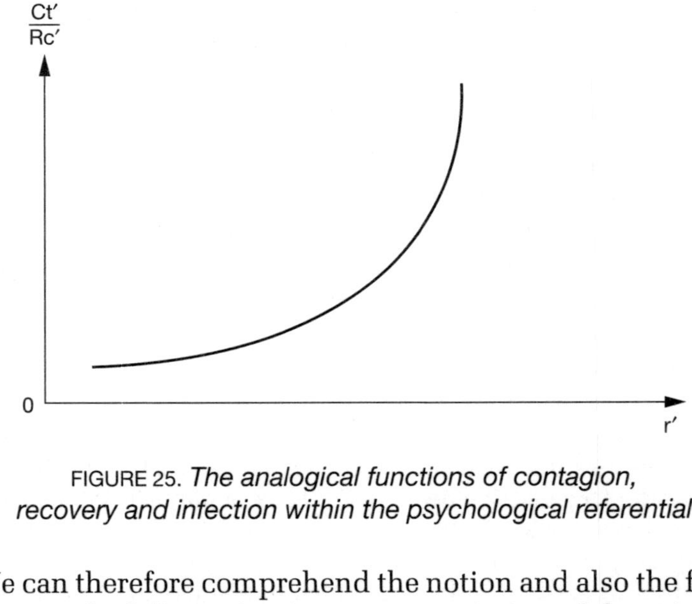

FIGURE 25. *The analogical functions of contagion, recovery and infection within the psychological referential*

We can therefore comprehend the notion and also the feeling of the speed of dissemination or transmission of the crisis. On observation, we are struck by the paralysing effect linked to the fact that the impact of the Covid crisis is very sudden and concentrated over a very short period (t_0 sequence). This:

(i) is consistent with the pattern of acceleration of the dissemination of the real virus within R_e;

(ii) is consistent with the pattern of acceleration of the dissemination of the initial image-objects $(io)_0$ within R. The latter is consistent, moreover, with the idea of an acceleration of the speed of circulation of the $(io)_0$ within R. The notions of $V_{(io)R}$ and r′ are similar. We are in fact comprehending a speed of circulation.

THE NOTION OF INTENSITY OF DISSEMINATION IN THE PSYCHOLOGICAL REFERENTIAL. THE COEFFICIENT Z_n

That is not all. There is a notion of the total population Pt, which is more or less completely infected. The more this population contracted the virus, the more probable it is that the virus will undergo a deceleration in *its own* circulation. What is the analogical equivalent for this in our description?

In the case of a real virus, there are people and individuals, who may or may not have been affected by the virus. In the analogy, there are indeed individuals who may or may not have been affected by a memory pattern (the image-object $(io)_0$). We may one day be able to know, for each individual, what happens (concerning what affects the individual but also about that which, in an innate or acquired manner, pre-exists even before the occurrence of the remembered pandemic, which brings with it those (io) which will interact with the innate or acquired (io)).

At this stage, we estimate the intensity with which the individuals are affected by the occurrences of (io) within the referential structures of the narratives (text, hypertext), calculations which digitalisation and big data now make possible on a large scale. By analogy with the total population Pt, we call a number or coefficient Z of occurrences which we hypothesize may be compared to a rate of dissemination of 100% of the population Pt′ (we are closer here to the notion of coming into contact with the virus, which is the image-object here, than to the strict notion of infection). Since Z corresponds to a rate of 100% of the population coming into contact with $(io)_0$, we then have Z′, Z″ … Z_n which represent the fractions of 100.

How can we then know, within the analogical analysis, that the population is more or less infected? The coefficient Z_n provides an answer as we have just seen.

A READING OF THE CRISIS USING Ct′/Rc′, r′ AND Z_n

We therefore have three important variables:

Ct′/Rc′ ; r′ ; Z_n

We can thus see that:

(i) if the initial image-objects $(io)_0$ continue to spread while accelerating, *i.e.* the *coefficient r′* of the number of new image-objects which have a hereditary link with the same identity and the same direction as the initial image-objects;

(ii) therefore, if Ct′/Rc′ continues to increase while accelerating;

(iii) if Z_n is low (which means that the total population has little immunity),

then there is a strong probability of an exponential configuration.

Observation of the Covid crisis reveals, after a sharp increase in the crisis which was concentrated in time, various sequences where r′, Ct′/Rc′ seem to decrease, which may mean that Z_n is already at a high level after the very first crisis sequences.

Moreover, is there an analogical equivalent for the notion of being asymptomatic? This would concern individuals or populations who are infected by the virus but whose symptoms are not observed. In our analogical approach, this could relate to objective occurrences of image-objects (and, therefore, to an actual exposure of individuals or populations to such image-objects), which are therefore included within Z_n, but which do not manifest themselves by means of declarations or actions consistent with the identity (the memory pattern) of such image-objects: for example, occurrences of $(io)_0$ which are properly accounted for within Z_n for which the narrative/action of individuals is different from $(io)_0$ (which would imply the ability to back the estimated occurrences with investigations); which would make it possible to explain the phenomena of a relapse of the crises after a first, initial recovery (the 2008 crisis, a rebound in 2020 at the time of the Covid crisis), since asymptomatic persons would be carriers of the initial, negative, zero image-objects but their behaviour would be inconsistent with this. In any event, this attempt to interpret asymptomatic cases will need to be refined further.

PART II

What do we mean by the fundamentals?

INTRODUCTION – THE MISCONCEPTION OF THE FUNDAMENTALS

By showing that, if the markets were rational, then share prices could and should be explained by some combination of anticipated dividends, R. Shiller and, moreover, the majority of commentators and observers, have concluded that market behaviour was irrational, or at least contained a certain dose of irrationality, or that rational situations were exceptions.

The term "irrational" only has meaning here by comparison with a notion of rationality which is posited, and above all defined, *ex ante* by a certain number of indicators, magnitudes and variables. This is true of the so-called value indicators for the stock markets which, as we have shown elsewhere (see *Carnets monétaires*; *Essays in Positive Investment Management*), only made a small contribution, in their usual definition, to explaining and in particularly to predicting movements in share prices, even at the extreme points.

This may be due to the imperfect or incorrect treatment of an otherwise relevant topic – and, also, the need to extricate oneself from irrelevant, cyclical noise when assessing value, e.g. for earnings which, everything suggests, should be relevant for an understanding of the stock markets, if they were handled better *i.e.* understood in their non-cyclical component, since, over a cycle, the distractions from opposing signs largely cancel each other out.

It may also be due to the ultimately irrelevant nature of the topic, even though it is considered, by both theory and practice, to be an essential element of understanding and modelling. It might, quite simply, transpire that we continue to look at, analyse and predict variables which only explain a very limited part of reality, or indeed none at all. Such a hypothesis would have several consequences: (i) other variables or dimensions would have been underestimated and should in turn be tested; this would either be an essential dimension in the treatment of an already identified topic, e.g. the phenomena of memory and forgetfulness incorporated into the analysis of earnings or other variables, which are, as it were, traditional when describing and predicting the stock markets, or a topic which at least appears to be different, e.g. the whole of the narratives which structure market behaviour like a discourse or, more generally, the hypothesis that we have made (see *La dynamique boursière – Les fondements*; which is taken up again in *Essays in Positive Investment Management*) according to which the risk premium of the stock market, far from merely reflecting the fundamentals that each person has in mind, of which company results constitute in symbolic terms the most visible and most commented element, represents, at any given time, an arbitrage between the shares *and everything else* and, consequently, contains a representation of the world and its areas of risk; in this last hypothesis, we are pointing out that the methodological bias of both theory and practice which only reads into the movements of stock markets, because they relate to companies, phenomena which are directly related to companies, does not do justice, in our hypothesis, to the functional nature of the market, which we have described as a form of consciousness which the modern world gives itself in order to appear to itself; (ii) consequently, the apparent ignorance or inefficiency of the so-called fundamentals (which are in fact only partly ignorant/inefficient or not at all so) would not point to a particular irrationality but would instead indicate a partial or even zero understanding of stock market movements.

The so-called fundamentals are in fact located at the heart of what should be called a misunderstanding. It is only because there is an *agreement*, in the manner of an act of faith or a convention, to recognise the existence of fundamentals which, *a fortiori*, would alone make it possible to have a rational understanding of share price movements, that we choose to describe a certain number of situations as contravening the fundamentals (there are in fact numerous descriptions of deviations from a fundamental reality). This leads to the idea that there is, on the one hand, a reality, that of the fundamentals and, on the other, transitory situations of deviations or misleading forms of appearances. Reality thus ceases to be described in a unitary and homogenous manner; the deviations are dismissed as irrational and excluded from scientific descriptions. They are literally without reason.

They probably only appear to be without reason because we have not yet managed to describe, in a unitary manner, the whole field of observed realities. However, there is a temptation to describe as irrational increasingly important swathes of the observed field.

THE PREMISE OF A RETURN TO THE FUNDAMENTALS

Reliance on the notion of a divergence or deviation from the fundamentals offers a deceptive, twofold comfort. It allows part of the observation to be eliminated by dismissing it as irrational (which proves to be more radical than a mere admission that it is incomprehensible, which would acknowledge that this field is of an ontological nature) and, above all, a return to the fundamentals to be posited, which is a return to equilibrium and, therefore, to justify a practical action plan based on such a prediction. Confidence in the self-correcting mechanisms (mean reversion) supports this approach.

The refusal to consider a field of observations which is broad but is defined as a set of transitory phenomena which distance or separate us from the fundamentals not only introduces an analytical bias of situations but also contains a self-fulfilling dimension, since numerous practical actions (prediction and execution) are undertaken *with* the idea of a future return to the fundamentals and to an equilibrium.

We have shown elsewhere (see *La Valeur. Substance, échange et prix*) how important it was, when stripping the former fundamentals of their substance, not to remove all references to a substance and thus precipitate the whole system into a complete irrationality.

CHAPTER 7

The two hypotheses for the reformulation of the fundamentals

We have essentially formed two types of major hypotheses.

THE HYPOTHESIS THAT THE FUNDAMENTALS AND THE RISK PREMIUM ARE COMPREHENSIVE

(1) The role of the markets, and the significance of this role, will only be very *partially* understood so long as our perspective and our analyses are only *partially* concerned with the sole, apparent topic which seems to constitute this field, largely limited to the central role played by companies in the equity market, which is accompanied by that played by a few other institutions and the variables associated therewith (the institution of central banks and interest rates represent the main ones).

This role is far more extensive, as we have shown (see *L'économie sociale de la liberté*; *The Social Economy of Freedom*). The market, in the modern era, is the conscious form adopted by society and the world in order to appear to themselves and, consequently, to transform themselves by acting. This transcendence constitutes the market as a (collective) Subject. This collective Subject, thus defined, has been the subject of far less attention and study than the individual Subject. And yet it is the actual, dominant form of this historical sequence of human societies.

Such a transcendence, once understood and accepted, naturally incorporates a far broader set of actors, variables and risk premia, in fact all of them. The complete set of risk premia and the connection in terms of projection and action towards that which is to come can be found within the gap or distance between the market and the world (society). The market gives a value at any one time to the whole of the action prospects and their risks.

There is, therefore, a combination of specific elements (e.g. company results) and a global premium which expresses a broader state of projection of society (the world) towards the future within the action (see *La dynamique boursière*).

If these premises are accepted, it must mean that the traditional market calculations of risk premia are extremely *partial*, that the element of global risk discussed should enable us to provide a better definition of the risk premium and reduce its mysteries.

The market as a transcendent form

The market as a transcendent form, which makes it possible to put a price on *all* the futures, implies that the choice of assets which it incorporates is the result of an arbitrage between such assets and *everything else*. This is why the risk premium is indeed greater than we thought. It is *all* the fundamentals of the world and of society which are at work and not just company fundamentals.

It follows that the consideration of company fundamentals is not necessarily an error but that, undoubtedly, (i) we are not looking at such specific fundamentals in the way that we should (we will come to this aspect in point 2 below), and (ii) there are many other matters involved.

THE HYPOTHESIS OF NARRATIVE STRUCTURES
AND A DISCOURSE FORMED BY MEMORY AND FORGETFULNESS

(2) For an understanding of the role and operation of the markets, we should take into account narrative structures which are sustained by the dynamics of memory and forgetfulness from a psychological referential whose substance is an economic time of duration which offers analogies with physical time and is even closer to a form of psychological time (see *Pure Theory of Economic Time. Rovelli-Simonian meditations*). The whole thing functions as a discourse.

It follows from this second hypothesis that, at the very least, a filter of this type must be applied to the traditional fundamentals (and, therefore, to company fundamentals) in order to avoid the risk that they do not tell us much and prove to be useless, thus justifying in return the idea that such elements are completely useless.

It also follows that such narrative patterns of memory and forgetfulness, whether fanciful or anchored in some form of reality, are worth researching as such, solely for their structural properties and *irrespective of the topics* which they fix, like images on a film. This is the price for exploring the territory of what we have called the global premium, over and above the specific, direct, company elements alone.

THE SPECIFIC RISK PREMIUM, THE GLOBAL RISK PREMIUM AND THE NARRATIVES

Overall, we accept that the market risk premium can be written as:

$$ERP = f(R_S, R_G, \alpha)$$

(see *La dynamique boursière. Les fondements*), *i.e.* the combination of (i) a so-called specific risk premium which incorporates a filter of duration, memory and forgetfulness, but also possibly the pure narrative elements concerning the matter constituted by companies without that necessarily concerning the traditional "fundamentals" for the analysis of such companies from the financial market viewpoint; and (ii) a global risk premium, whose subject matter cannot be specific, since this premium expresses an arbitrage between the representative assets of the relevant market and *everything else*. Such a global premium necessarily incorporates the dimensions of duration, memory and forgetfulness, together with the characteristic narratives.

From a practical viewpoint, and for each of these areas, the following actions can be considered:

Definition of the specific risk premium

(1) The specific risk premium will be written as a function of memory and forgetfulness of a relevant business activity variable (*i.e.* one element of the traditional fundamentals), together with a structure (pattern) of narratives which maintain a link between the matter and the company's direct topics. Such narratives must speak about the company but not necessarily or solely about that company's activity. On the contrary, all the possibilities of an imaginary world are incorporated here, structured by stories, discourses or what we call narratives. The developments arising from Big Data and AI will be put to use here, in order to identify and deal with such structures.

We have:

$RPE = f(srp_{(E)}, grp_{(E)})$

$srp_{(E)} = f((acorp)_{M/F}, (ncorp)_{M/F})$

where:

$(acorp)_{M/F}$ = a fundamental, synthetized element of the business activity adjusted by the effects of memory and forgetfulness within the psychological referential of duration,

$(ncorp)_{M/F}$ = the company's benchmark narrative(s).

In the search for the specific, fundamental element which is unique to the company, the company is described as a referential structured as an imaginary world and the combination (i) of the most immediate elements within perception, *i.e.* connected to the activity and the results – but which are themselves either placed within a perspective of memory, forgetfulness and duration, or treated as pure narratives linked to a reality or even more fanciful (pure narratives exist which are more or less fanciful surrounding, for example, the company's results, which occasionally form part, whether rightly or wrongly, of a long-term memory, and which therefore structure what can be called an imaginary, psychological referential of the business activity fundamentals –) and (ii) elements for which the final referential is, or involves, the company but which go far beyond the strict framework of its activity and its results (accordingly, a company sustains an imaginary referential and narratives which are much broader than a mere analysis of traditional fundamentals is willing to imply).

Definition of the global risk premium

(2) The global risk premium will be written as a combination of a global valuation point and a narrative (or a combination of narratives) which is itself global.

The approach adopted for the specific risk premium is, therefore, symmetrical. The idea is that there is a value dimension and a narrative dimension.

We have:

$RPE = f\,(srp_{(E)}, grp_{(E)})$

$grp_{(E)} = f\,(Vg_{M/F}, ng_{M/F})$

where:

$Vg_{M/F}$ = valuation of the global assets

$ng_{M/F}$ = global benchmark narrative

CHAPTER 8

The function of subjective value and of narration, the function of perceived risk

THE FUNDAMENTALS AS A PERCEIVED *VALUE* REFERENCE AND *NARRATIVE* STRUCTURE, WITH *SPECIFIC* AND *GLOBAL* DIMENSIONS

We associate, for a specific perimeter (that of companies for the stock markets) and for a global perimeter, *a value standard and a narrative structure.*

A market's fundamentals can be described as a *value* reference and a *narrative* structure, with two dimensions, one being a specific dimension for the immediate, principal market purpose and the other a global dimension, *i.e.* everything which does not come within the specific dimension defined above. *Value* is understood to mean the incorporation of a tangible, real reference element for each of the two dimensions (specific and global), such as company results, within a psychological referential structured by memory, forgetfulness and duration. This incorporation reflects the perspective from the economic Subject's viewpoint (or, for example, the investor's) with a displacement from a form of external, objective reality (in the traditional approaches to fundamental value) to an object of perception. This is a matter of perceived value, value "for myself". Perceived value is introduced into this definition, value as a fact of perception, the consideration of narratives relating to the object of the external, objective reality itself (e.g. here, the company results).

Narrative is understood to mean a structure (pattern) of discourse stemming from an imaginary world which may or may not have reference links with events or objects from the so-called objective reality.

We introduce *perception* firmly into the construction of the fundamentals, through perceived value and the narrative.

For RPE, we have the following type of function:

$$\text{RPE} = \alpha \, \text{srp}_{(E)} + \beta \, \text{grp}_{(E)}$$

And
$(\text{acorp})_{M/F} = x\ (\text{ncorp})_{M/F}$
$(\text{Vg})_{M/F} = y\ (\text{ng})_{M/F}$

We posit a link between the narrative structures and the perceived values, within both the specific and global dimensions.

As a result, perception is introduced into what is traditionally defined as a fundamental, objective matter. Fundamentals are always facts of perception.

It follows from this hypothesis that the fundamentals must be seen as a *function of value and narration* to which we can apply a few characteristics from Tversky's value function (see *The Essential Tversky*), including, in particular, an asymmetry of perception as between gains and losses, with concave forms for gains and convex forms for losses, and an emancipation from the constraints of the classical utility functions.

FUNDAMENTALS FOR THE SUBJECTIVE VALUE FUNCTION

Tversky's value function

We take from Tversky the idea that: "*The subjective value is a deviation from a reference point, therefore it can be expressed in terms of gains and losses.*"[1] And the risk is expressed in terms of gains and losses.

"The riskless component is the minimum gain or loss which is certain to be obtained or paid. The risky component is the additional gain or loss which is actually at stake."[2]

"The value of a strictly positive or strictly negative prospect equals the value of the riskless component plus the value-difference between the outcomes, multiplied by the weight associated with the more extreme outcome."[3]

"There are functions with concave and convex regions in both the positive and negative domains (of outcomes)."[4]

1. *"La valeur subjective est une déviation par rapport à un point de référence, elle peut donc être exprimée en termes de gains et de pertes."*
2. *"La composante sans risque est le gain minimal ou la perte minimale certains d'être obtenus ou payés. La composante risquée est le gain ou la perte supplémentaire qui est effectivement en jeu."*
3. *"La valeur d'une perspective strictement positive ou strictement négative est égale à la valeur de la composante sans risque majorée par la différence de valeur entre les résultats, multipliée par le poids associé au résultat le plus extrême."*
4. *"Il existe des fonctions avec des régions concaves et convexes à la fois dans les domaines positif et négatif (de résultats)."*

Representation of the subjective value function.
The perceived fundamentals

We describe RPE as a *subjective value function* containing 2×2 dimensions (which we call value; narrative; specific; global). It must be able to be expressed in terms of gains and losses. How can we move from the idea of perceived fundamentals to that of a subjective value function?

The fundamentals are said to be perceived, in our approach, if they are incorporated into a function of memory and forgetfulness (M/F) and, consequently, into a psychological referential of duration and economic temporality as we have defined the same. This is true of the example of a relevant variable for business activity. This may be enough to characterise a notion of value or fundamental value of a subjective nature.

This perception function is always there, if narrative structures (patterns) are incorporated into the analysis, such narratives being able to apply to (i) the business activity (the first dimension of the approach) and, more generally, to all topics concerning the company (dimension of specific fundamentals or specific value); (ii) *everything else* (the second dimension of the approach), from the viewpoint of the global assets and, more generally, to the global or general narratives which characterise what we have called the world or society in a relevant and significant manner (dimension of the global fundamentals or of global value).

We have $F_p = f\,(F_pS, F_pG)$

$V_s = f\,(V_sS, V_sG)$ et $V_s = a\,(V_sS + V_sS') + b\,(V_sG + V_sG')$

Where,

F_p = perceived fundamentals

V_s = subjective value and $F_p \sim V_s$

The F_p function has been used to construct the RPE function.

We make a hypothesis that F_p can be expressed as a function of "Tversky-style" subjective value. The fundamentals incorporated into a function of memory and forgetfulness (M/F) and, consequently, into a psychological referential (R), fluctuate around a reference point which can be seen as a point of equilibrium which constitutes a point of neutrality and equilibrium within a referential regime. We have shown that, at *equilibrium*, there is a neutrality of the effects of memory and forgetfulness or, if dynamic, an iso-distortion of the factors of memory and forgetfulness. *Absolute equilibrium* is a static situation, where time is absent, a situation which is not very realistic within the observable world. *Limited relative equilibrium* defines a situation of consistency or stability of the factors of memory and forgetfulness within the Subject's space-time referential. *Relative equilibrium*, which is more dynamic and realistic, includes the fluctuations of the said referential and, therefore, those of the factors of memory and forgetfulness.

This is also true of the example of supposed equality at equilibrium of savings and investment. This is only acceptable for functions of memory and forgetfulness which are neutral (*absolute equilibrium*) or consistent in their effects (*limited relative equilibrium*). The equality discussed above is a specific case of global equilibrium. In observed reality, there is a fluctuation of the factors of memory and forgetfulness and therefore multiple equilibria (*relative equilibrium*) which may appear as sub-equilibria. The relative dynamic of the Subject's spatio-temporal referential is dominant.[1]

Arguably, a link exists between the quantity of money and the value given to time. This does not mean that the quantity of money influences the value given to time (the latter would arguably decrease as the former increases). Instead, one accepts the idea that a modification of the value given to time means that an increase or decrease in the quantity of money has an impact on prices. Therefore, there is not necessarily a link between the quantity of money and inflation. There may be one *if* the movements of money are accompanied by modifications in the value given to time. The quantitative approach must therefore be increased by the value given to time. Economic policy action cannot ignore the value given to time. Accordingly, the so-called situations of a "liquidity trap" and the inefficiency of traditional actions may be understood by including the extreme distortion of the referential of value given to time.

There is, therefore, monetary neutrality, *i.e.* an increase in the means of payment which are not likely to cause disequilibria, including that of inflation, when, for a given growth of the monetary mass, the value given to time (or its distortion) is stable, this value being defined, in one way or another, on the basis of factors of forgetfulness and memory which are attached to real and financial variables within the referential. Monetary neutrality corresponds to a series of pairings, which combine

1. See *Essays in Positive Investment Management*, pp. 210-213.

a quantity of money and the value given to time, in level form and/or in variation, each pairing representing a state of the means of payment (or the growth thereof) for a given state of the Subject's psychological referential, which contains the structure of the value given to time. Monetary neutrality is defined in a relative manner within a relativist theory of the quantity of money.[1]

PERCEIVED FUNDAMENTALS AS PERCEIVED RISK IN TERMS OF GAINS AND LOSSES

Equilibrium of the fundamentals and neutrality of risk

The point of equilibrium, of reference and neutrality of the perceived fundamentals (of subjective value) corresponds to a perceived risk of neutral reference, *i.e.* (in the sense used by Tversky) corresponding to a lack of gains and losses. The $F_p(V_s)$ function incorporates the deviations from this point of reference. It is these deviations which give meaning and value to the notion of risk.

Taking a risk means moving away from a situation where the perceived fundamentals are compatible with a situation of "no gain or loss". A risk-free situation and, consequently, a risk-free asset is that for which the perceived fundamentals are compatible with the combination which associates minimum gain *and*, at the same time, maximum certainty, *i.e.* that which can be achieved with the highest degree of certainty.

Definition of equilibrium

Equilibrium can be defined as a situation:

(i) where there are no gains or losses; risk corresponds to a situation where (1) the existence of gains does *not* correspond to an absolute certainty of obtaining them, or (2), in a downgraded alternative, a situation where the existence of gains does not correspond to the greatest certainty of obtaining them – which implies that such gains would not be minimal – (3) or does not correspond to the lowest uncertainty that they will be obtained – which suggests that such an uncertainty would not be minimal –, (4) or does not correspond to the *accepted* uncertainty;

(ii) such a definition raises a number of questions and difficulties. There is a difference between *a lack of gains*

1. See *Essays in Positive Investment Management*, pp. 220-221.

and losses, an impossibility of further increasing gains, an impossibility of additional gains without a (more than proportionate) increase in losses, an impossibility of an additional (marginal) gain without realising a loss (see the theory of surplus and our works – *Value, Time and Capital* and also *Pure Theory of Economic Time*). Each of these situations may characterise an equilibrium;

(iii) numerous elements have to be taken into account: the existence of gains, the existence of losses, the certainty *attached* to the existence of gains and the existence of losses (of obtaining them, which introduces the idea of an *expected or anticipated existence*, or at the very least a perceived existence), *accepted* certainty for the same magnitudes, *perceived* certainty.

Dynamic process. Definition of zero or minimum risk

The reference point for the start of the dynamic process is, therefore, a situation where the risk (in light of the various hypotheses which we have just referred to) is either zero or objectively minimal, or psychologically minimal.

(i) The risk is zero when there are no gains or losses, which means:
(a) a situation where the existence of gains or losses is not recorded concomitantly, (b) where such an existence is *no longer* recorded, (c) a situation where such an existence is not, or is no longer, perceived, (d) a situation where such an (expected) existence is not, or is no longer, anticipated. The lack of gains or losses is not necessarily an absolute and objective situation but may, often, be relative (the rate of the absolute *increase* in gains and losses and in gains as compared to losses), or subjective, *i.e.* resulting from a psychological referential, and taking time into account (economic temporality, of a psychological nature and traditional temporality of the future and of anticipation).

(ii) The risk is objectively minimal when minimal gains exist, *i.e.* a concomitant objective observation, which are obtained with the highest possible level of certainty. This means, for a concomitant, objective observation:
(a) that it is impossible to make an additional gain without the appearance of (a1) a loss, (a2) a loss which is more than proportionate to the gain; it is specifically the idea of not downgrading the profile of "gains versus losses"

within a structure of an asymmetrical perception of gains and losses (one is willing to sacrifice gains in order to limit the losses) which ensures the highest possible certainty;
(b) that there exists (here) an objective level of gains and of losses, such levels not being zero and being able to take on significant, absolute values where the slowdown in the increase in gains (the reduction of gains) is accompanied by a more than proportionate slowdown in losses.

There is here a concomitant, objective observation, which means that there are no hypotheses made for the future (it is not a question of anticipated gains or losses in a future which is, consequently and by definition, uncertain), nor regarding the real or perceived nature of the gains and losses (it is a question of real magnitudes), nor the nature of the certainty concerning the gains and losses (it is still a question of realities and not of perceptions which may require correction).

A low or even minimal risk may characterise a high, absolute level of gains provided that (a) the absolute level of losses is itself low or even minimal (in this situation, the notion of certainty attached to the idea of a minimum level of gains for the highest level of certainty corresponds to the low, objectively-recorded losses); (b) the marginal increase in objective gains recorded with a real certainty within the immediate, concomitant present (*i.e.* which marks the on-going action without referring to the notion of a future and, therefore, of an anticipation) is accompanied by a marginal increase in losses which are more than proportionately lower (proportionately stronger marginal decrease).

Similarly, within this line of reasoning, the notion of a certain level of real, recorded uncertainty can replace that of a real (high) certainty which accompanies the aforementioned relationships between gains and losses.

There is, therefore, a relationship between gains, losses and certainty.

(iii) The risk is psychologically minimal when all the preceding propositions characterise a psychological referential of anticipation, perception, expectation and acceptation and, in particular, the variables of gains, losses and certainty; when the future exists for the projected on-going action; when the uncertainty is dominant and perceived, not real.

This essentially means (a) situations where the perceived gains (perception encompasses here all the notions discussed in the preceding paragraph) are high for low, perceived losses and a level of perceived uncertainty which is itself low; (b) situations where the marginal, anticipated increase in gains does not result in a marginal, more than proportionate, rise in losses. This may characterise high, initial, absolute levels of gains or/ and losses.

We have therefore identified three categories of situations, where the risk is zero, where the risk is objectively minimal and where the risk is psychologically minimal.

We have the following "r" risk functions:

(i) r_0,
(ii) $r_{obj(min)}$,
(iii) $r_{psy(min)}$,

and functions of perceived fundamentals and subjective value:

(i) $F_p = f\,(F_pS, F_pG)$,
(ii) $V_s = f\,(V_sS, V_sG)$
$V_s = a\,(V_sS + V_sS') + b\,(V_sG + V_sG')$.

CHAPTER 9

Representation of objective and perceived risk (gains and losses) and function of subjective value and of narration

RISK, GAINS AND LOSSES, AND (UN)CERTAINTY

In this approach, up to now, there are three interconnected notions which seem self-evident but which pose problems.

It is said that the *risk* is minimal for *gains* which are themselves minimal and which can be obtained with a maximum degree of *certainty*.

(i) *Risk* is defined by the *gains/losses* pairing, and by it alone, which corresponds to a certain limited definition of the investor utility function, of the choice and preference function, (ii) it is, above all, a question of risk and not of uncertainty, which connects the reasoning to the possibility of observation and of the measurement of (past) occurrences, (iii) but the risk itself is linked to the notion of certainty (and uncertainty), since the latter characterises the gains (and losses). What certainty are we talking about? What can it be based on, if not some past statistical recurrence; we then have a definition of risk based on certainty and uncertainty which, in addition to the comparison of two notions from different dimensions and of different natures (risk is the measurement of the past for the purposes of a future projection, uncertainty is undoubtedly closer to a pure contingency), instrumentalizes the notion of what is certain or uncertain while undermining it. Consequently, the notion of "risk-free" is close, in this Tversky-style analysis, to that of certainty (about the gains, here) and, consequently, an increase in risk is defined by an increase in uncertainty, which amounts to mixing the two notions.

Here, risk is a function of (un)certainty (regarding the gains).

The situation of a lack of risk is theoretical in a fundamentally uncertain world (unless one removes the hypothesis of uncertainty). Risk can be defined by uncertainty, the notions must be distinguished and separated.

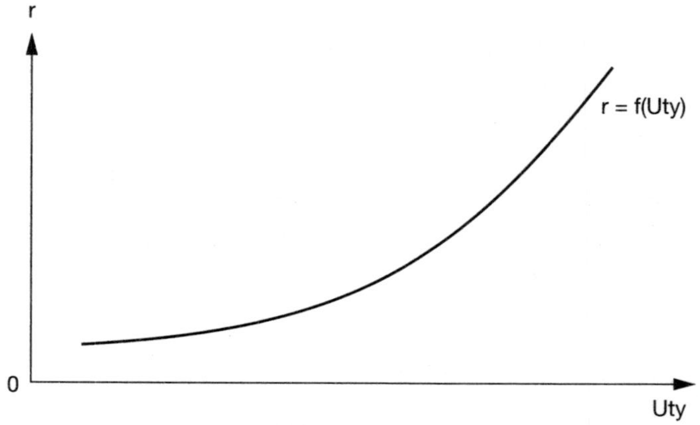

FIGURE 26. *Risk as a function of uncertainty regarding the gains*

Risk is a fact of perception, uncertainty is a fact of materiality (in what circumstances can we speak of "perceived uncertainty"?).

REPRESENTATION OF THE THREE RISK FUNCTIONS AND THE TWO FUNCTIONS OF PERCEIVED FUNDAMENTALS AND SUBJECTIVE VALUE

We have three risk functions and two functions of perceived fundamentals and subjective value which are united.

First representation. Integration of a function of gains, losses and objective risks and a function of subjective value

(1) First representation:

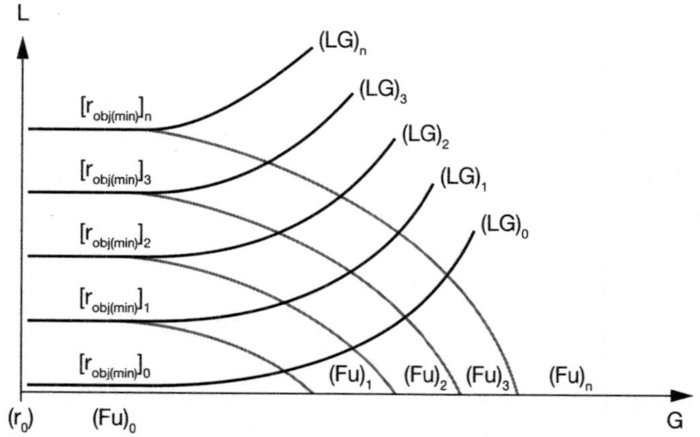

FIGURE 27. *First representation of the functions of risk and of perceived fundamentals (subjective value)*

Where $(LG) = f((r_0), [r_{obj(min)}]_n, LG_n) \sim (F_{obj}) \sim F_p(V_s)$
Where G = gains and L = losses (*losses*).
r_0 = no gains or losses observed.

LG = rate of relative increase of gains and losses. It can be seen that the flat part of (LG) corresponds to those situations where there is a rise in gains without an additional increase in losses. This flat part of (LG) can be compared to the idea of a zero or minimal risk (*i.e.* $[r_{obj(min)}]$ where $[r_{obj(min)}] \geq (r_0)$).

A graphic representation is provided here of the first two risk functions, namely (r_0) and $[r_{obj(min)}]$, for functions of objective gains and losses (*i.e.* recorded and not perceived, projected or anticipated – see below the distinction between the objective and psychological risk functions; it can be estimated that we mean, by the term objective, a referential of certainty and of a perpetual present and, by psychological, we mean a referential of uncertainty and an apprehension about the future), namely L, G and (LG).

There is also a $[F_p(V_s)]$ function of perceived fundamentals (of subjective value) whose equilibrium point of reference and neutrality, as seen above, corresponds to a perceived risk of neutral reference, *i.e.* the absence of gains and losses, the latter here being understood as objective in the sense in which we have defined the functions L, G and (LG).

A risk is taken as soon as one moves away from this region of equilibrium.

In this first representation, we thus graft (1) a function of subjective value $[F_p(V_s)]$ (2) onto an objective referential of, first, functions of gains and losses (L, G, (LG)) and, second, of risk functions $(r_0, r_{obj(min)})$.

We make the hypothesis that:

(i) the function $(r_0, [r_{obj(min)}], LG)$ constitutes an acceptable approximation for the function of perceived fundamentals or of subjective value $[F_p(V_s)]$;

(ii) the purely theoretical (non-observable) function of the objective fundamentals, if it exists, is itself close to (i).

The subjective value (perceived fundamentals) function makes it possible to:

- provide a better explanation for the objective (recorded) trajectory of the function of gains and losses (LG) and, consequently, that of market behaviour;
- explain the disconnection between what are called fundamentals (within the usual definition which is given to them) and market behaviour, but also between theoretical fundamentals which are supposed to be perfectly estimated and

that same market behaviour, unless we consider that no such fundamentals exist as we imagine them (*i.e.* based on real, purely economic variables) and that they are, in real life, replaced by subjective value. Not only would the fundamentals which are usually commented upon explain very little but even a function of pure fundamentals, if one were to exist, would do no better than $F_p(V_s)$.

There are three functions of fundamentals:

(i) the function of objective fundamentals (F_{obj}), *i.e.* the function which would best *explain* market behaviour and the profiles of gains and losses based on the traditional elements for the valuation of such markets, *at the expense of an adequate treatment* of the latter. This function, which does not exist today or is not observable, is the subject of a sort of quest for the Holy Grail, or at least for references (the fundamentals, *i.e.* those which would be able to explain).
These objective fundamentals, if they were to exist or were observable, would abolish the gap between what is recorded of the evolution of the markets and the discourse which consists of saying that "this is not supported by the fundamentals". It would be a justification of what is observed by a function of elements which up to now are described as fundamentals, *i.e.* the real elements directly linked to the market components.
Such objective fundamentals, which are non-observable or have not yet been observed, would justify asset price trajectories which seem, up to now, to be irrational.
Such a function, by pushing the realms of logic, is in keeping with a rationale of efficiency. (F_{obj}) is that which at any given time is reflected in the prices;

(ii) the function of usual fundamentals (F_u), *i.e.* all the valuation indicators used by the participants, which we know cannot explain the majority of movements, even at the extreme points, which explains why (F_u) is almost always out of sync with the observed trajectories of gains, losses and prices;

(iii) the function of perceived fundamentals $F_p(V_s)$ and of subjective value which we have defined, which can be thought to best explain observed gains, losses and prices but based on a definition of such fundamentals which is both expanded (value and narratives, specific and global) and projected into a psychological time of memory and forgetfulness (M/F). N.B.: the function (F_{obj}) can itself also incorporate a projection into the future starting from M/F, but based on the usual components, such as Shiller's approach for the valuation of the PER (CAPE).

At the end of this first representation, we obtain a simple model of objective gains and losses approximated by a function of perceived fundamentals and not the function of usual fundamentals adopted by market practitioners. We maintain the hypothesis that a function of objective fundamentals exists which would treat the usual elements in such a way that they would provide a perfect explanation for objective gains, losses and prices. The functions (F_u), $F_p(V_s)$ and (F_{obj}) present a flat part which corresponds to minimal risk.

One of the special features of this first representation is the choice of objective functions of gains and losses, *i.e.* of true, recorded gains or losses. We now make a hypothesis of *perceived* gains and losses.

Introduction of the hypothesis of perceived *gains and losses*

(2) Second representation:

We are now focussing on a (LG_p) function. It involves, first, linking the risk functions r_0 and $r_{psy(min)}$ and, second, the fundamentals functions $F_p(V_s)$ and (F_u) and, finally, the perceived gains and losses function (LG_p). We leave aside, for the moment, the objective functions (F_{obj}) and $r_{obj(min)}$.

We are, therefore, within a (M/F)-style psychological referential. Risk is no longer expressed in terms of gains and losses (Tversky) but in terms of *perceived* gains and losses – and, by perceived, we mean projected or anticipated within a psychological referential where perception, and together with it the notion of the future, is approximated by memory, forgetfulness and duration.

The risk is, shall we say, a perceived risk within such a referential. The perceived risk of neutral reference corresponds to the lack of *perceived* gains and losses. The departures from the reference neutrality represent the *perceived* risk, namely $r_{0(p)}$ and $r_{psy(min)}$.

The (LG) and (LG_p) functions must logically be different, at least in part, although it should be noted that a $r_{obj} = f\ (r_{psy})$ link exists, in the sense that the perception of risk may constitute a significant part (in a causal sense) of the recorded, objective risk, *i.e.* that the perception of risk reduces the latter (negative relationship) or, on the contrary, reinforces its appearance (positive relationship of a self-fulfilling type). We have $r_{obj} = \pm a (r_{psy})$.

Tversky teaches us that there is:

(i) a preference for certain gains (with a high degree of certainty);

(ii) a preference for probable losses (with a high degree of probability).

Gains are particularly desirable if they are more sure/certain.

Whether gains or losses, there is a preference for what is particularly certain. There is a steeper value curve for losses than for gains. Loss aversion is stronger than appetite for gain for the same amount of loss or gain.

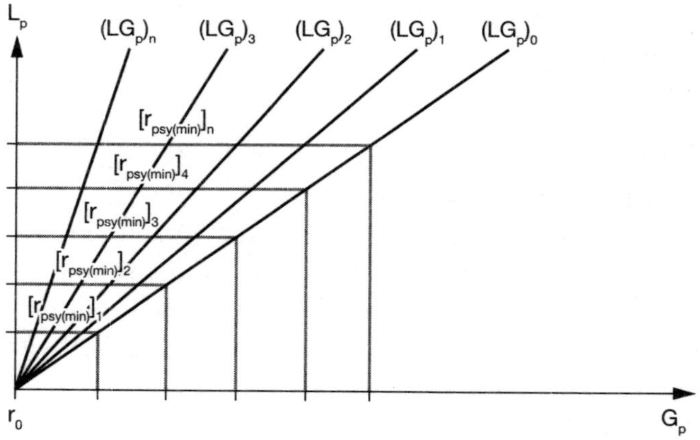

FIGURE 28. *Second representation of the functions of risk, of fundamentals, of perceived gains and losses*

CHAPTER 10

Reformulation of the (LG) and $(LG_p)_n$ functions of objective and perceived gains and losses

THE FOUNDATIONS OF THE FUNCTION OF GAINS AND LOSSES (LG)

The (LG) function was constructed with the following ideas:

(i) the rate of relative increase of gains and losses. What matters is the relative value and trajectory and, in particular, whether the marginal unit of increase in gains produces an increase in losses which is more than proportionate, rather than the absolute values taken separately from the gains and losses. We have defined a point zero (no gains or losses) and a risk function $[r_{obj(min)}]$ which describes those situations where there is an increase in gains without an increase in losses (or without an increase in losses which is more than proportionate, which constitutes a second interpretation), *i.e.* the flat part of the curve (LG), which describes a relative, minimal risk (and not an absolute risk as for r_0);

(ii) the hypothesis that the (LG) function follows a very pronounced curve of acceleration with an almost vertical, exponential profile, reflecting that the marginal units of gains produce losses in an acceleration which is more than proportionate. This point can be verified using objective data, since we find ourselves with (LG) within a representation of objective (recorded) gains and losses;

(iii) the hypothesis that the $F_p(V_s)$ function of perceived fundamentals or subjective value has a form which is close to that of (LG).

THE (LG_p) FUNCTION (*PERCEIVED* GAINS AND LOSSES). FOUR HYPOTHESES

The (LG_p) function introduces the following, additional ideas and hypotheses:

(1) Aversion to loss is stronger than appetite for gain for the same amount of loss or gain. The $(LG_p)_n$ curves are located to the left of a neutral function $(LG_p)_0$. Within this region of the graphic representation, the additional, marginal unit of perceived gain implies an increase in perceived losses which is more than proportionate.

(2) The absolute, perceived risk $(r_0)_p$ corresponds to a lack of perceived gains and losses.

(3) There are situations where the increase in perceived gain is not accompanied by any increase in perceived losses (or any increase which is more than proportionate). These situations correspond to a relative, perceived, minimal risk, noted as $r_{psy(min)}$.

(a) Hypothesis (1) (aversion to loss is more important than appetite for gain for the same amount of gain or loss) excludes, in principle, those situations located to the right of $(LG_p)_0$ (there are indeed situations to the right of this curve where there is an increase in perceived gains for stable, perceived losses or a rise in losses which is less than proportionate but, in principle, such situations contravene hypothesis (1)).

(b) By adhering to the hypothesis, *i.e.* by placing oneself to the left of $(LG_p)_0$, situations can be observed where, by moving over the flat parts $[r_{psy(min)}]_n$, there is indeed an increase in perceived gains for perceived losses which are stable or an increase in perceived gains which is more than proportionate when compared to the perceived losses. This is true within the limits of $(LG_p)_0$ and bearing in mind that, even so, there are some situations which are located in a region which is consistent with hypothesis (1).

(4) It seems reasonable to make a hypothesis that the $(LG_p)_n$ curves acquire a very curved, exponential and almost vertical form, which corresponds to those situations where there is no longer any perceived gain for infinite, perceived losses.

NEW REPRESENTATION OF THE $(LG_p)_n$ FUNCTIONS AND CURVES

Based on this, we can provide a new representation of the $(LG_p)_n$ curves.

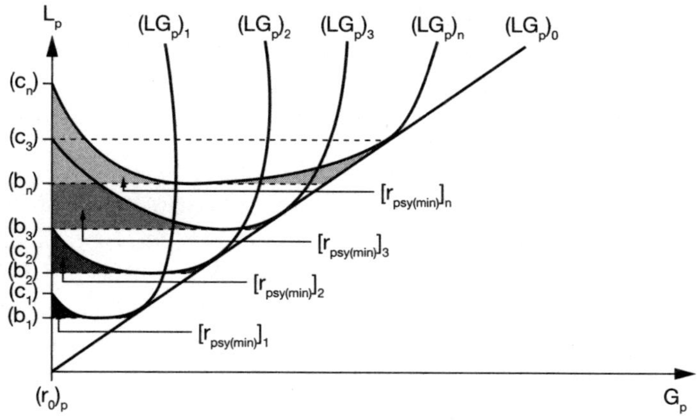

FIGURE 29. *Third representation of the $(LG_p)_n$ functions of perceived gains and losses*

Characteristics of the $(LG_p)_n$ curves

We are describing the $(LG_p)_n$ curves which have the following characteristics:

(i) one part which describes situations where the perceived gains rise in a manner which is more than proportionate to the perceived losses. Situations can even be envisaged where, relatively speaking, the perceived losses diminish. The form of this first part may, therefore, be (a) immediately increasing, (b) flat or (c) descending. (b) and (c) are situations of relative minimal risk. If minimal risk is defined, as we have, by a non-increase in perceived losses for a rise in perceived gains, then (a) is not part of $[r_{psy(min)}]_n$. If there is a non-increase in perceived losses, which is more than proportionate, then (a) can be accepted;

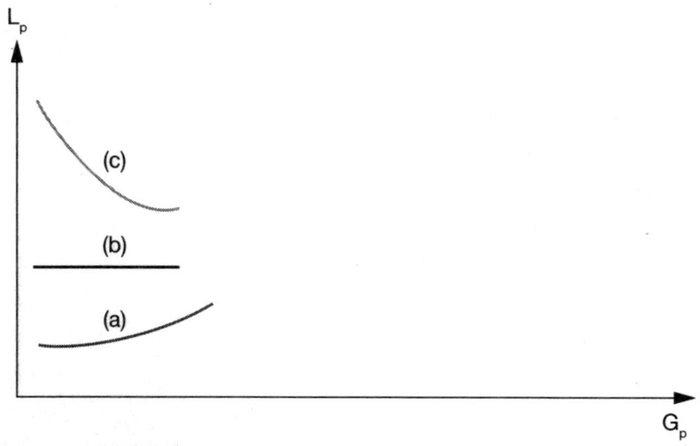

FIGURE 30. *Characteristics of the $(LG_p)_n$ functions and curves*

(ii) one part with an accelerating recovery for an almost vertical profile, illustrating that the marginal unit of perceived gains is accompanied by an exponential rise in perceived losses;
(iii) a point (or surface) of contact with the neutrality curve $(LG_p)_0$.

By comparison with the first representation:
(i) (LG_p) is constrained by hypothesis (1) (see (a)), *i.e.* by the consideration of a psychological referential and established behavioural facts. (LG) was not constrained, on the assumption that it was objective (it is supposed to represent what is recorded of the distribution of gains and losses through historical observation).

Importance of analysing the real *distribution of the gains and losses*

Two consequences follow from this.
(a) An analysis of this *real* distribution cannot confirm the hypothesis made above, which would then mean that, even though the psychological referential requires hypothesis (1) to be taken into account, *i.e.* the perceptive asymmetry between gains and losses, the observation of the actual distribution of such gains and losses within real life does not truly validate this hypothesis. This leads to difficulties in incorporating the (LG) and (LG_p) functions (this will be one of the subjects of the third representation):
Either we posit that (LG_p) is an adaptive function of (LG) and hypothesis (1) will ultimately collapse or diminish. (LG_p) and (LG) converge with a causal effect of (LG) on (LG_p).
Or the two functions remain separate and unconnected: real life within R_{phy} (real referential) is radically different from that which prevails in R_{psy} (psychological referential) and participants continue to be confronted with objective occurrences which differ from their bias or anticipations. This may provide an explanation for volatility and shocks, and for the difficulty which participants face in forming anticipations (even without the volatility of such anticipations). The psychological referential is regularly caught off guard, or in default, by what is actually going on. We are not far-removed from a market efficiency hypothesis faced with which participants can do nothing. A new definition of risk is revealed there, as a gap between (LG_p) and (LG). *Taking a risk means distancing oneself from (LG)* which results in a form of minimal risk.

Or we posit that (LG_p) produces (LG), which constitutes a paradox since, after all, the two functions are distinct. In such a case, it is the very structure of perceptive asymmetry between gains and losses which would lead to a different distribution as a result of the many attitudinal biases it would give rise to.

(b) An analysis of the real distribution may, on the contrary, validate hypothesis (1). It follows that:

- the two functions are integrated;
- the objective distribution of gains and losses can be explained by their structure of perception;
- accordingly, there is no reason, by extension of reasoning to the more general question of market behaviour, to consider solely the traditional fundamentals alone. It is even open to question whether they are of any analytical use. It can be argued that gains, losses and prices are, essentially, the product of perceptive structures. In any event, there would be an explanation for the gap between what is recorded and the fundamentals.

It can be seen that the question of the relationships between, first, objective gains and losses and, second, perceived gains and losses is an important one. We should be able to make progress by developing and refining each of their measurements.

GRAPHIC REPRESENTATIONS

We break the (LG) function down into $(LG)_{n'}$ and $(LG)_{n''}$ separated by $(LG_p)_0$. No (LG_p) exists for the $(LG)_{n''}$ function, since the latter is located to the right of $(LG_p)_0$.

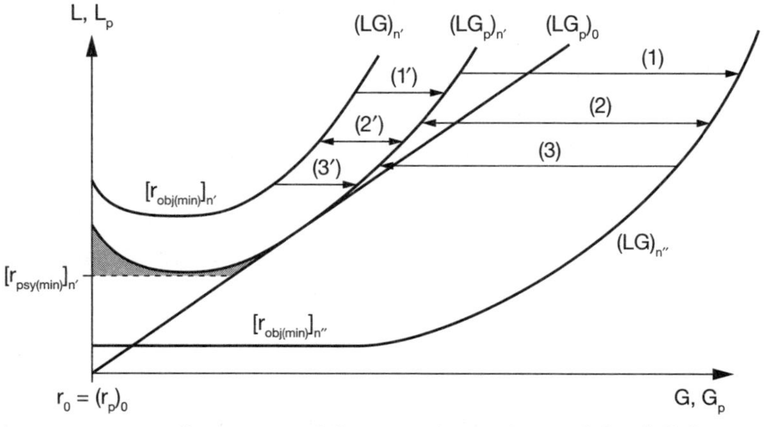

FIGURE 31. *Summary of the representations of the $(LG_p)_n$ functions of perceived gains and losses*

We note G and G_p on the horizontal axis and L and L_p on the vertical axis.

The two axes intersect at a point zero, where we can make a hypothesis that $(r_0) = (r_p)_0$. The total lack of objective (recorded) gains and losses and the total lack of perceived gains and losses do not overlap but the lack of objective gains and losses corresponds to a point where one can be sure that the lack of perceived gains and losses is corroborated by observed reality.

HYPOTHESIS (i)(a)

The principal relationship is between $(LG_p)_{n'}$ and $(LG_p)_{n''}$.

We note the three examples of the relative trajectories of $(LG)_{n'}$ and $(LG_p)_{n'}$ which are envisaged in (i)(a).

They are noted as ←, ↔, →.

HYPOTHESIS (i)(b)

$(LG)_{n''}$ does not exist here. We are to the left of $(LG_p)_0$.

The principal example of the trajectory is (1′).

Since the perceived losses are *always* greater than the perceived gains for the same amount of gain or loss, the perceived, minimal risk $[r_{psy(min)}]_n$ is relative, as it characterises situations (part of the (LG_p) curve) where the perceived gains increase while the perceived losses are unchanged (or the perceived gains undergo a proportionate increase which is greater than the perceived losses, *i.e.* there is an increase in perceived losses which is less than proportionate for a marginal, unitary increase in perceived gains) but these perceived gains remain less than the perceived losses in absolute terms.

We mean by this that the perceived minimal risk is itself also constrained and is biased, exposing the stakeholder to more complete, objective (LG) functions. The paradox is that the asymmetric perception of losses and gains, which should protect the stakeholder, instead exposes it to the disparity between $(LG)_n$ and $(LG_p)_n$.

Consequently, the true risk for the stakeholder, or total risk $[r_{tot}]$, is that which incorporates the risk functions $[r_{obj}]$ and $[r_{psy}]$ and corresponds to the $[LG/LG_p]_n$ disparity. A total, minimum risk exists for this integrated function.

$$[r_{tot}] = f\,([r_{obj}], [r_{psy}]) = f\,((LG/LG_p)_n)$$

$$[r_{0tot(min)}] = f\,([r_{obj(min)}, r_{psy(min)}])$$

The total, minimal risk must correspond to part of the $(LG/LG_p)_n$ curve.

Bibliography

Akerlof, G.A. and Shiller, R. (2009), *Animal Spirits: How Human Psychology Drives the Economy and Why It Matters for Global Capitalism*, Princeton University Press.

Allais, M. (2001), *Fondements de la dynamique monétaire*, Paris, Éd. Clément Juglar.

Barberis, N. and Thaler, R. (2003), "A Survey of Behavioral Finance", in Constantinides G.M., Harris, M. and Stolz, R.M. (eds.), *Handbook of the Economics of Finance: Financial Markets and Asset Pricing*, Vol. 1, Chapter 18, 1053-1128, Elsevier/North-Holland.

Barthalon, E. (2014), *Uncertainty, Expectations and Financial Instability - Reviving Allais's Lost Theory of Psychological Time*, Columbia University Press.

Becker, G. (1976), *The Economic Approach to Human Behavior*, University of Chicago Press.

Bergson, H. (1st ed. 1939) (2008), *Matière et Mémoire*, Paris, collection Quadrige, PUF; (1994), *Matter and Memory*, English translation by Paul, N.M. and Scott Palmer, W., London, Allen & Unwin.

Bernoulli, D. (1738) (1954), "Exposition of a New Theory on the Measurement of Risk", translated from Latin by Sommer, L., *Econometrica* 22, n°1: 23-36.

Blanqué, P. (2009), *La dynamique boursière. Les fondements*, Paris, Economica.

Blanqué, P. (2009), *Théorie globale de l'intérêt, du cycle et de la mémoire*, Paris, Economica.

Blanqué, P. (2010), *Money, Memory and Asset Prices*, Paris, Economica (distr. Brookings Institution).

Blanqué, P. (2008), *Carnets monétaires*, Paris, Economica.

Blanqué, P. (2011), *L'économie sociale de la liberté*, Paris, Economica.

Blanqué, P. (2011), *The Social Economy of Freedom*, Paris, Economica (distr. Brookings Institution).

Blanqué, P. (2012), *La Valeur. Substance, échange et prix*, Paris, Economica.

Blanqué, P. (1st ed. 2014) (2nd ed. 2016) (3rd ed. 2019), *Essays in Positive Investment Management*, Paris, Economica (distr. Brookings Institution).

Blanqué, P. (2018), *The Economic and Financial Order,* Paris, Economica (distr. Brookings Institution).

Blanqué, P. (2019), *Valeur, Temps et Capital,* Paris, Economica.

Blanqué, P. (2019), *Value, Time and Capital*, Paris, Economica.

Blanqué, P. (2020), *Théorie pure du temps économique. Méditations rovelli-simoniennes*, Paris, Economica.

Blanqué, P. (2020), *Pure Theory of Economic Time. Rovelli-simonian meditations*, Paris, Economica.

Buonomano, D. (2017), *Your Brain is a Time Machine: The Neuroscience and Physics of Time*, New York, Norton.

Camerer, C., Loewenstein, G. and Prelec, D. (2005), "Neuroeconomics: How neuroscience can inform economics", *Journal of Economic Literature*, Vol. 43, 9-64.

Constantinides, G.M. (1990), "Habit Formation: A Resolution of the Equity Premium Puzzle", *Journal of Political Economy* 98, June, 519-543.

Damasio, A., Tranel, D. and Damasio, H. (1990), "Face agnosia and the neural substrates of Memory", *Annual Reviews in Neuroscience*, Vol. 13, p. 89-109.

Deleuze, G. (1st ed. 1985), *L'image-temps*, Paris, Éditions de Minuit; (1989), *The Time-Image*, English translation by Tomlinson, H. and Galeta, R., Minneapolis, Minnesota Press.

Fisher, I. (1st ed. 1932), *Booms and Depressions. Some First Pirnciples*, New York, Adelphi Company.

Glimcher, P.W. (2011), *Foundations of Neuroeconomic Analysis,* Oxford University Press.

Hansen, L.P., Sargent, T.J. and Tallarini Jr, T.D. (1993), *Pessimism, Neurosis and Feelings about Risk in General Equilibrium*, University of Chicago, Working Paper, October.

Hayek, F.A. (1st ed. 1952), *The Sensory Order, An Inquiry into the Foundations of Theoretical Psychology,* Chicago, Illinois, The University of Chicago Press; (2001), *L'Ordre sensoriel*, Paris, CNRS éditions.

Hicks, J.R. (1973), *Capital and Time, A Neo-Austrian Theory*, Oxford University Press; (French translation) (1975), *Le Temps et le Capital*, translated by Glais, M., Paris, Economica.

Hogarth, R.M. and Reder, M.W. (eds.) (1987), *Rational Choice: The Contrast Between Economics and Psychology*, Chicago, University of Chicago Press.

Husserl, E. (1928), *Vorlesungen zur Phänomenologie des inneren Zeitbewusstseins*, Halle, Niemeyer; (1990), *On the Phenomenology of the Consciousness of Internal Time*, English translation by Brough, J.B., Dordrecht, Kluwer; (1st ed. 1964) (1996), *Leçons pour une phénoménologie de la conscience intime du temps*, Paris, PUF.

James, W. (1884), "What is an emotion?", *Mind*, Vol. IX (34), 188-205.

James, W. (1890), *The Principles of Psychology*, New York, Henry Holt and Company.

Kahneman, D. (2009), "The Myth of Risk Attitudes", *Journal of Portfolio Management.*

Kahneman, D., Slovic, P. and Tversky, A. (1982), *Judgment under Uncertainty: Heuristics and Biases*, New York, Cambridge University Press.

Kahneman, D. and Tversky, A. (eds.) (2000), *Choices, Values and Frames*, Cambridge UK, Cambridge University Press.

Knight, F.H. (1921), *Risk, Uncertainty, and Profit,* New York, Houghton Mifflin.

Knutson, B., Taylor, J., Kaufman, M.T., Peterson, R. and Glover, G. (2005), "Distributed neural representation of expected value", *Journal of Neuroscience*, Vol. 25, 4806-4812.

Kuhnen, C.M. and Knutson, B. (2005), "The neural basis of financial risk-taking", *Neuron*, Vol. 47, 763-770.

Lo, A.W. (2017), *Adaptive Markets*, Princeton University Press.

Mandelbrot, B. and Hudson, R.L. (2004), *The (Mis)Behaviour of Markets: A Fractal View of Risk, Ruin and Reward*, Basic Books.

Merleau-Ponty, M. (1st ed. 1942) (4th ed. 2013), *La structure du comportement*, Paris, PUF; (1963), *The Structure of Behavior*, English translation by Fisher, A.L., Boston, Beacon Press.

Merleau-Ponty, M. (1st ed. 1945), *Phénoménologie de la perception*, Paris, Gallimard; (1962), *Phenomenology of Perception*, English translation by Smith, C., New York, Humanities Press.

Merleau-Ponty, M. (2011), *Le monde sensible et le monde de l'expression*, Cours au Collège de France, Notes (1953), MétisPresses.

Patinkin, D. (1965), *Money, Interest and Prices: An Integration of Monetary and Value Theory*, 2nd ed., New York, Harper & Row.

Rovelli, C. (2017), *L'Ordine del tempo,* Ed. Adelphi.

Sartre, J.-P. (1st ed. 1936), *L'imagination*, Paris, Gallimard; (2012), *The Imagination*, English translation by Willford, K. and Rudrauf, D., London, Routledge.

Sartre, J.-P. (1st ed. 1939), *Esquisse d'une théorie des émotions,* Éd. Hermann, Paris; (1948), *The Emotions: Outline of a Theory*, English translation by Frechtman, B., New York, Philosophical Library.

Sartre, J.-P. (1st ed. 1940), *L'imaginaire*, Paris, Gallimard; (2004), *The Imaginary*, English translation by Webber, J., London, Routledge.

Shiller, R.J. (1989) (1992), *Market Volatility*, MIT Press.

Shiller, R. (2000) (2005), *Irrational Exuberance*, Princeton University Press.

Shiller, R. (2003), *The New Financial Order: Risk in the 21st Century*, Princeton University Press.

Shiller, R. (2019), *Narrative Economics – How Stories Go Viral & Drive Major Economic Events*, Princeton University Press.

Shiller, R. (2019), Online Event LSE, 20 September 2020.

Simon, H.A. (1957), *Models of Man, Social and Rational: Mathematical Essays on Rational Human Behavior in a Social Setting*, Oxford, Wiley.

Simon, H. (1979), *Models of Thought*, Yale University Press.

Taleb, N.N. (2007), *The Black Swan: The Impact of the Highly Improbable*, Penguin Books.

Thaler, R. (1991) (1994), *Quasi Rational Economics*, New York, Russell Sage Foundation.

Thaler, R. (2015), *Misbehaving: The Making of Behavioral Economics*, New York, W.W. Norton & Company.

Tobin, J. (1958), "Liquidity Preference as Behavior Towards Risk", *Review of Economic Studies*.

Tversky, A. (2018), *The Essential Tversky*, MIT Press.

von Mises, L. (1st ed. 1912, German), *Theorie des Geldes und der Umlaufsmittel*; (1934, London) (1981), *The Theory of Money and Credit*, Indianapolis, Liberty Fund.

von Mises, L. (1st ed. 1949, English) (4th ed. 1996), *Human Action: A Treatise on Economics*, Indianapolis, Liberty Fund (5 vol).

Table of figures

TABLE OF CONTENTS

PART II
What do we mean by the fundamentals?